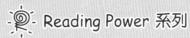

Reading Power 系列

Advanced

閱讀經典文學時光之旅：美國篇

附解析本

陳彰範・編著

三民書局

國家圖書館出版品預行編目資料

閱讀經典文學時光之旅：美國篇／陳彰範編著．——初版一刷．——臺北市：三民，2019
面；　公分

ISBN 978–957–14–6617–0　（平裝）
1.美國文學 2.文學評論

874.2　　　　　　　　　　　　　108004793

© 　閱讀經典文學時光之旅：美國篇

編 著 者	陳彰範
責任編輯	林雅清　潘盈吟
美術編輯	王立涵
內頁繪圖	江正一

發 行 人	劉振強
著作財產權人	三民書局股份有限公司
發 行 所	三民書局股份有限公司
	地址　臺北市復興北路386號
	電話　(02)25006600
	郵撥帳號　0009998–5
門 市 部	(復北店)臺北市復興北路386號
	(重南店)臺北市重慶南路一段61號

| 出版日期 | 初版一刷　2019年5月 |
| 編　　號 | S 807140 |

行政院新聞局登記證局版臺業字第○二○○號

有著作權．不准侵害

ISBN　978–957–14–6617–0　（平裝）

http://www.sanmin.com.tw　三民網路書店

序言

　　美國文學在世界文學的輿圖上，比起中國、印度、歐洲大陸、英國、俄國和阿拉伯，崛起甚晚。十七世紀早期先有原住民的口語傳統，接著是清教徒佈道式的敘述、擬仿歐陸傳說軼事的說書，和建國前後擘劃未來願景的論述。

　　新大陸的人有清教徒自律堅韌的精神，以及對拓荒探險的執著。他們當然也面臨社會改革、教育醫療、金融重組，乃至奴隸制度廢除等問題。有批思想家和作家樂觀地認為，世界不分鉅細各自有存在的意義，且神性存於每個角落。只要提供機遇，人皆能展現無限的潛力。然而有截然不同的思維也在美國文學中浮現，勾勒內心幽微深處，靈魂不安的悸動：虛偽、傲慢、邪惡、內疚、貪婪等人性的醜陋，也成了作品探索的主題。

　　為了讓讀者淺嘗美國文學心靈的饗宴，我們依時序選擇了八篇作品，主要以敘事文類為主，取其情節，旨在使讀者在閱讀中體認隱含其間的人生哲理。對原著的改寫盡可能維持作品初始的風貌，但難免有不少精彩內容流失，我們於賞析和 Something You Should Know 裡略加補充。選文更結合重要的議題，如《自傳》強調自我品德素養的提昇，進而關懷社會改革和服務。《最後一個摩希根人》則是尊重美洲原住民，增進跨越族群間的相互瞭解。美國大陸座落在兩大洋之間，海洋世界時而寧靜時而洶湧的特性，暗指人性善惡兼備。人類野心未必能征服自然的力量，這是《白鯨記》提示人們的教訓。《歡樂谷傳奇》雖然描繪的是理想社會的願景，但書中人物對性別平等的價值，和性別權力關係認識的偏頗，最終導致理想的幻滅。《頑童歷險記》探索個人的良心與傳統社會的價值，那一個比較重要？從哈克對吉姆同情的態度可以看出端倪。家庭和學校的良好的互動，可以培育青少年健全的人格發展，正向鼓勵其發揮所長，這是〈保羅案例：一樁青春氣質的研究〉留給讀者省思的課題。身體的苦痛與心理的折磨，有些能隨時間流逝慢慢遺忘，有些卻需更多的包容與反思，身心才能得到療癒。〈大雙心河〉強調人與自然結合，才有重獲新生的可能。〈畜棚焚毀〉則處理親子關係，故事裡的父親粗暴專橫，喪失對他人的尊重，最後也禍及自己的親人。

　　這部經典選集在眾人的協助下完成：從原著的改編到英文編輯部同仁的費心投入，皆是集子問世的功臣，藉此感謝他們的付出。我們期待有心透過經典文學提升英語能力的讀者，能從書中得到樂趣和啟發。若有缺漏或謬誤之處，尚祈雅正。

陳乾範

· 使用說明 ·

關於作者
介紹作者的生平、寫作風格及著作等。

年表
以垂直年表列出作者生平的重大事件。

相關資料補充
關於作者或作品的相關資料、圖片補充。

**Words for Production
Words for Recognition
Idioms and Phrases**
列出重要單字片語的英標與中文解釋。

朗讀音檔音軌
每篇故事分別有一段完整及三段分段的朗讀音檔,以及單字朗讀音檔。

精選字彙
精選文章中重要單字片語,並標以粗體與註碼,或以不同顏色做標記。

Something You Should Know
補充說明故事背景的小知識,或解釋原書內的重要段落,協助讀者進一步理解作品。

Discussion
以討論開放式問題,引領讀者思辨。

課後練習題

閱讀測驗、字彙填充及引導式翻譯三大題協助讀者理解文章與練習運用單字片語。

賞析

針對文本做更深入的說明、分析，協助讀者更理解作品。

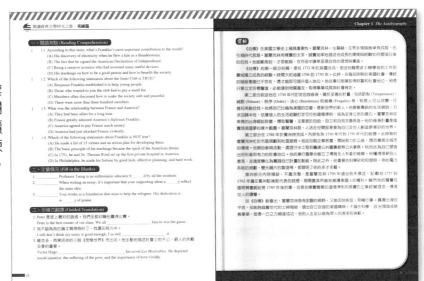

解析本

提供文本翻譯、練習題解析與答案。

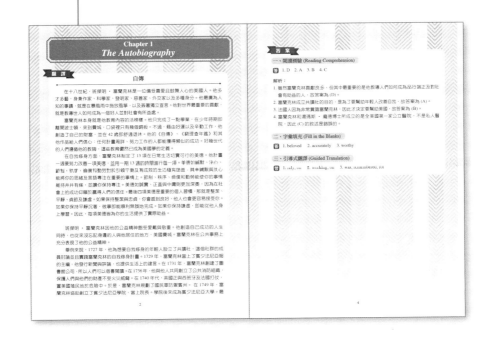

·線上音檔下載教學·

邊聽邊讀，聽故事學習英文更有趣！
用「聽」的方式，增強你的閱讀力！

STEP 1.　前往「三民東大英文學習網」→「學習素材」→「英語學習素材」下載。
http://www.grandeast.com.tw/englishsite/Mterial?T=263

STEP 2.　進入頁面後，點選想要書籍，進行下載。

閱讀經典文學時光
之旅：美國篇

學習素材

 英語學習教材

STEP3.　下載完成後，會取得一個 zip 檔。

閱讀經典文學時光之旅：美
國篇(內無文字檔，限購買　　下載
此書者下載)

STEP 4.　解壓縮檔案，依據提示輸入指定密碼，即可取得音檔。

Track 1　　Track 1-1　　Track 1-2　　Track 1-3

Track 2　　Track 2-1　　Track 2-2　　Track 2-3

音檔分成完整音檔及分段音
檔兩種模式。檔名按照章節
排列，Track 1、Track 2 等
為完整音檔；Track 1-1、
Track 1-2、Track 1-3 等
為每章節的分段音檔，皆分
三段。讀者可依需求自行選
擇不同音檔下載。
另有單字朗讀音檔！

Track 3　　Track 3-1　　Track 3-2　　Track 3-3

Track 4　　Track 4-1　　Track 4-2　　Track 4-3

密碼提示：
Chapter 4 第 12 個單字。

Contents ★ ★ ★

Chapter 1

The Autobiography

關於作者

　　班傑明・富蘭克林 (Benjamin Franklin, 1706–1790) 在許多領域皆成就非凡。年少時，先是憑藉自己的努力在印刷業闖出名號，接著開始從事公益活動，將想法付諸行動改善大眾生活。良好的溝通與協調能力使他能周旋於不同團體間，解決內政問題。而後更成為駐英的賓州代表，努力爭取美國殖民地的利益，協助草擬美國獨立宣言 (The Declaration of Independence) 及參與憲法的撰寫。他在科學研究的成果也享譽國際，著名設計如避雷針。早期從事印刷業，讓他有機會發表對政治和社會議題的看法；而後他也經常審視自己的一生，在 1771 年開始記錄過去，寫下個人的經歷，成為《自傳》的初稿。

　　他善於處事之道，寫作不求功名，旨在教育大眾成為好公民。他探索的主題包括：個人成功仰賴勤奮、儉約、節制；堅持公理正義的價值，用人唯才，無視特權和地位；肯定正直品格及自我修身。除了為州政府撰寫的文字莊嚴高雅外，其餘文類他堅持用語簡單。平日筆端流露出溫馨真誠，但是遇上社會重大課題時，他的文字即變得犀利如匕首，切中時弊。其次，他執筆糾舉社會弊端時，常用諷刺方式處理議題，展現其過人的學養、機智和幽默。小品則常以書信的文體呈現，最有名的一篇是〈蜉蝣〉(“The Ephemera”) 描述作者自己化身為短命的蜉蝣，長期陷在無聊的政治和科學的領域，早已失去生命的意義。這是少數展示富蘭克林悲觀面的作品。《窮理查年鑑》(*Poor Richard's Almanack*) 的說書人化身為卑微的小人物，最後成了極有哲理、講究道德的人。書裡除了記載每日的星象變化，內容也加入警句、格言、詩行、民間傳統和諺語。

　　他的《自傳》栩栩如生地描述少時離家到賓州費城的故事，先是經營印刷業致富，而後獻身公益活動與政治，致力改善居住的城市及國家。此書之所以變成大眾喜愛的作品，在於其展示勵志成功的範例。他精闢的箴言以及反躬自省、追求高尚品德的態度是世人珍貴的遺產。

▲富蘭克林 (中間) 操作印刷機。

富蘭克林年表

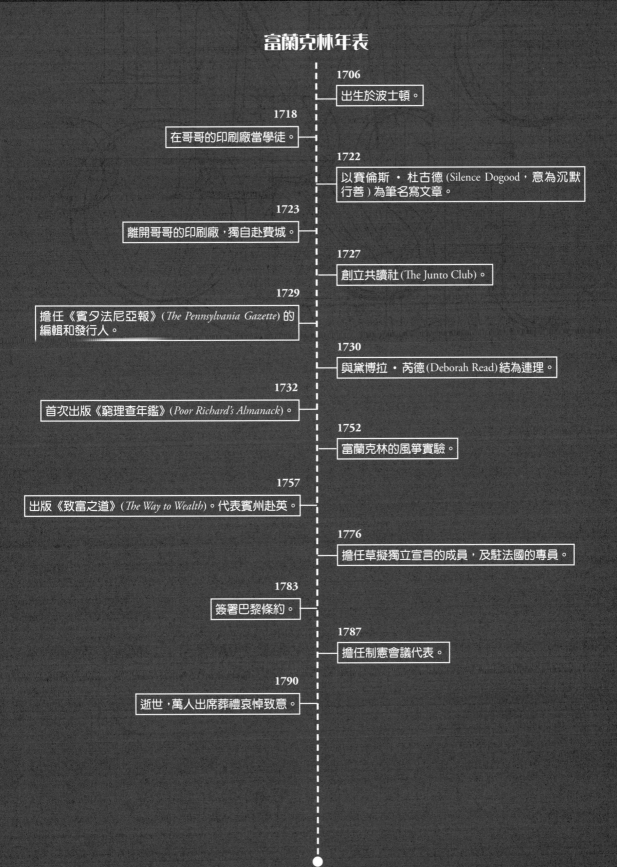

1706
出生於波士頓。

1718
在哥哥的印刷廠當學徒。

1722
以賽倫斯・杜古德 (Silence Dogood，意為沉默行善) 為筆名寫文章。

1723
離開哥哥的印刷廠，獨自赴費城。

1727
創立共讀社 (The Junto Club)。

1729
擔任《賓夕法尼亞報》(*The Pennsylvania Gazette*) 的編輯和發行人。

1730
與黛博拉・芮德(Deborah Read)結為連理。

1732
首次出版《窮理查年鑑》(*Poor Richard's Almanack*)。

1752
富蘭克林的風箏實驗。

1757
出版《致富之道》(*The Way to Wealth*)。代表賓州赴英。

1776
擔任草擬獨立宣言的成員，及駐法國的專員。

1783
簽署巴黎條約。

1787
擔任制憲會議代表。

1790
逝世，萬人出席葬禮哀悼致意。

課文朗讀 完整 Track 1／分段 Track 1-1

Benjamin Franklin was a **beloved**[1] and inspiring American of the 18th century. He was **versatile**[2]: he was a writer, scientist, inventor, public benefactor*, **diplomat**[3] and more. He was best remembered for flying a kite during a thunderstorm and signing the **Declaration**[4] of Independence. His most important contribution to the world was his **teachings**[5] on how to be a good person and how to benefit society.

Franklin himself was living proof of his teachings. He left Boston as a teenager with little education and went to Philadelphia with only a few coins in his pocket. However, by good luck and hard work, he made his fortune and retired comfortably by the age of 42. His *Autobiography*, *Poor Richard's Almanack** and other writings gave people confidence that anyone who plans well and works hard could achieve similar success. Many generations of people have followed his teachings, which came to define the American Dream.

For self-improvement, Franklin developed 13 virtues that were practical in daily life. The plan was to work on one virtue for a week, and all in a 13-week cycle. Virtues like silence, resolution, **temperance**[6], order, frugality* and **industry**[7] are useful for leading a balanced and **productive**[8] life. Silence and resolution can keep your thoughts and words on the important things. Temperance, order, frugality and industry can keep your things in good order and keep you focused. Virtues like sincerity, justice and **moderation**[9] are deeper, for success in society depends on winning people's trust. The

---

Something You Should Know

富蘭克林、美國夢 (The American Dream) 與資本主義

　　富蘭克林的《自傳》是塑造美國民族精神的重要著作。書中的箴言與勵志語成為美國人上進奮鬥的圭臬，他描繪的願景成了富庶繁榮的啟示，而他的獨立與自信成了美國人日常奉行的標竿。他鼓勵大眾改變環境、掌握機會，相信在平等公開的社會，每個人皆能發揮潛力，展現長才，這正是美國夢的精髓：勤奮工作和篤實待人，新大陸的人皆可獲得物質滿足、經濟保障，及社會尊重。

　　政治經濟學家馬克斯・韋伯 (Max Weber, 1864–1920) 在《新教倫理與資本主義精神》(*The Protestant Ethic and the Spirit of Capitalism*) 中說明：現代社會生產力的提升，有部分是源於勞動階級對自身工作的熱忱，並不全然是對利益的追逐。韋伯認為熱忱及以自己的工作為傲，是刻苦自律的新教徒精神。韋伯也特別推崇誠實、節儉和審慎，認為它們是值得信賴之人的必備條件，也是成功的資本主義體系不可或缺的要素。富蘭克林早在韋伯之前，在《自傳》(*The Autobiography*) 和《致富之道》(*The Way to Wealth*) 裡即大力鼓吹個人聆聽心中的呼喚，勤奮自立及積累財富是為了追求更好的明天。韋伯與富蘭克林有相同的信念：人有責任完成自己的任務，而勤勞和簡樸是致富的基礎。若韋伯認定這是資本主義精神，富蘭克林毫無疑問為此精神身體力行的楷模。

final four virtues are important personal habits, that is, cleanliness, tranquility*, chastity*, and humility*. If you are clean and chaste, you will feel good and other people will accept you easily. If you stay calm, you will do things smoothly and **accurately**[10]. If you stay humble, you can learn from others. Thus, all of the virtues offer practical benefits for your life.

▲ 〈班傑明・富蘭克林從空中引電〉(*Benjamin Franklin Drawing Electricity from the Sky*)。

Words for Production

1. beloved [bɪ`lʌvɪd] *adj.* 熱愛的，被喜愛的
2. versatile [`vɝsətl̩] *adj.* 多才的
3. diplomat [`dɪplə‚mæt] *n.* [C] 外交官
4. declaration [‚dɛklə`reʃən] *n.* [C] 宣言
5. teachings [`titʃɪŋz] *n.* [plural] 教誨
6. temperance [`tɛmprəns] *n.* [U] 節制
7. industry [`ɪndəstrɪ] *n.* [U] 勤勞
8. productive [prə`dʌktɪv] *adj.* 豐收的；有生產力的
9. moderation [‚mɑdə`reʃən] *n.* [U] 適度
10. accurately [`ækjərɪtlɪ] *adv.* 正確地

Words for Recognition

*benefactor [`bɛnə‚fæktɚ] *n.* [C] 捐助者
*Almanack [`ɔlmə‚næk] *n.* [C] 年鑑
*frugality [fru`gælətɪ] *n.* [U] 節約；樸素
*tranquility [træn`kwɪlətɪ] *n.* [U] 平靜，安寧
*chastity [`tʃæstətɪ] *n.* [U] 純潔，貞潔
*humility [hju`mɪlətɪ] *n.* [U] 謙遜

Idioms and Phrases

1. be remembered for sth 因⋯而成名；因⋯被記得
2. work on sth 努力改善；致力
3. depend on 依靠

★ ★ ★
Discussion

Do you agree with Franklin on his view that virtues were worth pursuing because of its practical benefits?

課文朗讀 分段 Track 1-2

Benjamin Franklin was loved and respected for his public spirit. While creating his own successful life, he always thought of the people and the place where he lived: Philadelphia, America. Franklin addressed his public spirit most vividly in his public projects.

For instance, in 1727, he set up the Junto Club. It was a club for young people who wanted to improve themselves. The club members discussed and followed Franklin's self-improvement plan. In 1729, Franklin served as the chief editor of the *Pennsylvania Gazette*. He published news and critiques* and also offered advice on effective living. In 1731, Franklin founded the Library Company so people could borrow books to read. In 1736, he **co-founded**[11] the Union Fire Company to protect people and property from fires. In the 1740s, England was fighting Spain and France. This put the American colonies in danger. So, Franklin planned a military force to defend Pennsylvania. In 1749, Franklin established the Public **Academy**[12] of Pennsylvania and served as its head. This academy later became the University of Pennsylvania. Finally, in 1751, Franklin and Dr. Thomas Bond founded the Pennsylvania Hospital. It was the first public hospital in the American colonies. Franklin showed his public spirit in public projects that served the needs of society.

In **midlife**[13], Franklin learned how to do scientific experiments. His most famous

Something You Should Know

Hitherto I had stuck to my resolution of not eating animal food, and on this occasion consider'd, with my master Tryon, the taking every fish as a kind of unprovoked murder, since none of them had, or ever could do us any injury that might justify the slaughter. All this seemed very reasonable. But I had formerly been a great lover of fish... when the fish were opened, I saw smaller fish taken out of their stomachs; then thought I, "If you eat one another, I don't see why we mayn't eat you." So I din'd upon cod very heartily... So convenient a thing it is to be a reasonable creature, since it enables one to find or make a reason for everything one has a mind to do. (The Autobiography, 1793)

富蘭克林的散文簡潔俐落且幽默風趣。這段原文摘錄還顯現他務實的個性。雖然講究原則，但也能通權達變。例如，他在一次旅遊中見到許多新鮮捕獲的鱈魚，他原決心不吃肉，覺得魚未曾傷害人類，實在沒有理由宰殺牠們。只是他從前一向喜歡吃魚，難敵香味撲鼻的誘惑。他在原則和嗜好間力求平衡，想起有一回見到剖開的魚肚內藏有許多小魚，心想既然牠們可以互吃，為什麼他不能吃牠們？他總結：人是講理的，只要有心辦事，總能找出理由。就算理念高遠，嗜好也不能置之不理，講道理前還得先填飽肚子。道德和世間事其實沒什麼不同，人得取中庸之道。

scientific discovery was proving that lightning was electricity. He also invented lightning rods* to protect buildings and ships from being struck. For his many contributions to science, the British Royal Society awarded him a **prestigious**[14] medal.

Because of Franklin's good reputation, the Pennsylvania government sent him to England to argue for American rights. His diplomatic efforts were much appreciated in America. In 1776, Franklin was sent to France to represent America. In France, Franklin wasn't just a diplomat; the French people were interested in him, including his style and his ideas. European scientists and thinkers visited him to discuss science and inventions.

Words for Production

11. co-found [ko faʊnd] *v.* 共同創立
12. academy [əˋkædəmɪ] *n.* [C] 學院；專科學校
13. midlife [ˋmɪd͵laɪf] *n.* [U] 中年
14. prestigious [prɛsˋtidʒəs] *adj.* 有聲望的，著名的

Words for Recognition

*critique [krɪˋtik] *n.* [C] [U] 評論
*lightning rod [ˋlaɪtnɪŋ͵rɑd] *n.* [C] 避雷針

Idioms and Phrases

4. set up 設立

★ ★ ★
Discussion

Franklin's passion for improvement was not on himself only. He also turned his attention to public projects. Which projects do you find most impressive and interesting? Why?

Benjamin Franklin was a man of confidence and **optimism**[15]. He believed these **characteristics**[16] were important for personal success. In his writings, he spread confidence and optimism. In his public projects, he showed the public that the needs of the society could be met. He showed people that if they meet life's challenges with confidence and clear thinking, they should feel optimistic of success. The basic principle of Franklin's teachings is that everyone has the opportunity of making such improvements. This principle became the spirit of the American Dream.

The American Dream is the faith that anyone who works hard and deals honestly will achieve **prosperity**[17], security and respect. Hard work leads a path to success. This path might not be short or easy, but anyone who works hard and grasps the right opportunities well can hope to succeed.

Franklin's *Autobiography* also taught the readers to respect the lowest citizens as equally **worthy**[18] as the wealthiest ones because they have the **potential**[19] to achieve the same success. Franklin also thought that poverty was bad only if one did nothing about it. He further stressed that young people could learn by themselves if they could

---

Something You Should Know

Keimer wore his beard at full length, because somewhere in the Mosaic law it is said, "Thou shalt not mar the corners of thy beard." He likewise kept the Seventh day Sabbath; and these two points were essentials with him. I dislik'd both, but agreed to admit them upon condition of his adopting the doctrine of using no animal food. "I doubt," said he, "my constitution will not bear that." I assur'd him it would, and that he would be the better for it. He was usually a great glutton, and I promised myself some diversion in half starving him. He agreed to try the practice, if I would keep him company. I did so, and we held it for three months... I went on pleasantly, but poor Keimer suffered grievously, tired of the project, long'd for the flesh-pots of Egypt, and order'd a roast pig. He invited me and two women friends to dine with him; but, it being brought too soon upon table, he could not resist the temptation, and ate the whole before we came. (The Autobiography, 1793)

這段摘錄顯示富蘭克林對人物的觀察入微，寥寥幾筆就能勾勒凱莫 (Keimer) 好辯貪吃的模樣。凱莫一向逞口舌之便，交談之間急要人聽命於他。凱莫喜歡富蘭克林的辯才，希望能和他合組宗教社。富蘭克林說，除非兩人在教義的詮釋取得共識，否則很難合作。例如，他同意凱莫蓄留長髮和鬍子、猶太安息日在星期六；但是，凱莫也得齋戒吃素。富蘭克林清楚他喜好葷食，決心用此考驗凱莫能堅持多久。雙方同意改變飲食習慣三個月，期間富蘭克林如魚得水，認為餐飲費用減少；凱莫卻覺得十分難受。有一天，凱莫晚餐訂了一份烤乳豬，邀請富蘭克林和兩位女士一同享用。沒想到當天烤乳豬提早上桌，幾位客人尚未到場，盤上的烤乳豬早已全進了凱莫的肚子裡。

not go to school. This lesson encouraged Abraham Lincoln to study law books at home. Lincoln later became an example of people's unlimited* horizons in America. Importantly, Franklin's messages made people feel confident in their own worth and optimistic of success even when life is hard. His teachings made people view America as a land of opportunities. Franklin's message of individual effort and social responsibility are two of the longest threads in the **fabric**[20] of American life.

▲ 五人小組 (亞當斯、富蘭克林、傑佛遜、李文斯頓、謝爾曼) 將獨立宣言上呈大陸議會。

Words for Production

15. optimism [`ɑptə,mɪzəm] *n.* 樂觀
16. characteristic [,kærəktə`rɪstɪk] *n.* [C] 特徵
17. prosperity [prɑs`pɛrətɪ] *n.* [U] 繁榮
18. worthy [`wɝðɪ] *adj.* 值得的
19. potential [pə`tɛnʃəl] *n.* [U] 潛力
20. fabric [`fæbrɪk] *n.* [C] 織品；結構

Words for Recognition

*unlimited [ʌn`lɪmɪtɪd] *adj.* 無邊無際的，無限的

★ ★ ★
Discussion

What do you think of Franklin's thought that what was best for the individual would in the long run be best for the mass?

一、閱讀測驗 (Reading Comprehension)

(　　) 1. According to this story, what's Franklin's most important contribution to the world?

    (A) His discovery of electricity when he flew a kite in a thunderstorm.

    (B) The fact that he signed the American Declaration of Independence.

    (C) Being a creative inventor who had invented many useful devices.

    (D) His teachings on how to be a good person and how to benefit the society.

(　　) 2. Which of the following statements about the Junto Club is TRUE?

    (A) Benjamin Franklin established it to help young people.

    (B) Those who wanted to join the club had to pay a small fee.

    (C) Members often discussed how to make the society safe and peaceful.

    (D) There were more than three hundred members.

(　　) 3. What was the relationship between France and America?

    (A) They had been allies for a long time.

    (B) France greatly admired America's diplomat Franklin.

    (C) America agreed to pay France much money.

    (D) America had just attacked France violently.

(　　) 4. Which of the following statements about Franklin is NOT true?

    (A) He made a list of 13 virtues and an action plan for developing them.

    (B) The basic principle of his teachings became the spirit of the American dream.

    (C) In 1751, he and Dr. Thomas Bond set up the first private hospital in America.

    (D) In Philadelphia, he made his fortune by good luck, effective planning, and hard work.

二、字彙填充 (Fill in the Blanks)

1. ＿＿＿＿＿＿＿＿ Professor Tseng is an enthusiastic educator b＿＿＿＿＿d by all her students.

2. ＿＿＿＿＿＿＿＿ When writing an essay, it's important that your supporting ideas a＿＿＿＿＿y reflect the main idea.

3. ＿＿＿＿＿＿＿＿ Tom works in a foundation that aims to help the refugees. His dedication is w＿＿＿＿＿y of praise.

三、引導式翻譯 (Guided Translation)

1. Peter 是班上最好的跑者。我們全都仰賴他贏得比賽。

    Peter is the best runner of our class. We all ＿＿＿＿＿＿ ＿＿＿＿＿＿ him to win the game.

2. 我不認為我的論文寫得夠好了，我還在努力中。

    I still don't think my essay is good enough; I'm still ＿＿＿＿＿＿ ＿＿＿＿＿＿ it.

3. 維克多・雨果因他的小說《悲慘世界》而出名。他生動地描述社會上的不公、窮人的苦難及愛的重要。

    Victor Hugo ＿＿＿＿＿＿ ＿＿＿＿＿＿ ＿＿＿＿＿＿ his novel Les Misérables. He depicted social injustice, the suffering of the poor, and the importance of love vividly.

賞析

《自傳》在美國文學史上極具重要性。富蘭克林一生顯赫,在眾多領域皆卓有成就,也引領時代思潮。富蘭克林用樸實的文字,誠實坦率地描述他成長的環境與經驗如何塑造日後的自我。他細膩周到、才思敏銳,在作品中謙卑呈現自我的理想與價值。

《自傳》的第一部分初稿,是在 1771 年於英國完成,敘述他離開波士頓學徒的工作到費城獨立成長的經驗。時間大約涵蓋 1706 到 1730 年。此時,在殖民時期的美國社會,傳統的階級意識已不存在,憑才能即可提升個人地位。他從事印刷業取得財富和社會地位,相信只要立定目標奮進,必能達到物質富足,取得事業成就與社會肯定。

第二部分敘述他在 1730 年代訂定自我修身、臻於至善的計畫,包括節制 (Temperance)、緘默 (Silence)、秩序 (Order)、決心 (Resolution) 和儉樸 (Frugality) 等,相信人可以改變、行善和再創自我。他將自己比喻為美國的亞當,是新世界的新人。他摒棄傳統的生活規訓,力求回歸本性,依據個人的生活經驗訂定可行的道德準則,做為安身立命的礎石。富蘭克林從卑微的出身崛起致富,博取聲譽,主要源於自助、自立和自我完善再造。他的修身計畫是個實現美國夢的偉大藍圖。富蘭克林說,人活在世間即是要為自己及世人創造更美好的世界。

第三部分在 1788 年於賓州時完成。內容包含 1730 年代到 1750 年代的經歷。此時期的富蘭克林忙於市區規劃和社區服務。他從印刷企業致富,開始致力於公益,想改善居住城市的環境。他親自參與活動,處理汙水工程和籌建公共圖書館等公共事務。他因此為自己塑造出好形象和有力的社會地位。他的善行義舉也樹立了博雅全人形象的楷模。他懂得接納別人意見,並適度轉化為實踐自己計畫的動能。除此之外,他重要的科學研究和發明,例如電力系統的規劃、雙光鏡片的製造等,都證明了他的多才多藝。

第四部分內容殘缺,不盡完整,是富蘭克林 1790 年過世前所撰述,記載他 1757 到 1762 年擔任賓州駐倫敦代表的經歷,期間盡其所能地維護美國人的權利。雖然他的聲譽在國際舞臺崛起是 1760 年後的事,但是他樸實簡單的道德準則和務實的企業經營理念,博得世人的讚譽。

從《自傳》能看出,富蘭克林既有宏觀的視野,又能因地制宜、見機行事。貧寒出身的平民,卻能跨越舊世代的士紳階級,譜出自立自強的美國精神。不論在科學、政治領域或慈善事業,皆憑一己之力順遂成功,他的人生足以做為眾人的表率和典範。

The Last of the Mohicans

關於作者

　　詹姆斯・菲尼莫爾・庫柏 (James Fenimore Cooper, 1789–1851) 在文學的成就非凡。他筆下的歷史傳奇、拓荒和海洋小說皆對浪漫主義有極大貢獻。有人認為他是最早推動生態意識的作家，例如在《拓荒者》(*The Pioneers*) 裡顯現環境保護的重要。後人創作的西部開發的故事或電影，不少是受到庫柏的啟發。

　　庫柏在作品的故事開端常摘錄喜愛作家的名言佳句。他擅長在人物的背後，陪襯恢宏的史觀或壯麗的地景。他先以全景呈現地貌，然後逐漸縮小範圍聚焦在小團體或單一人物。雖身處紳士階級，但是他卻能掌握社會低階平民的言行舉止。偶爾在故事中穿插風趣諺語；敘事雖偶有偏離主題的缺失，但他總能創造驚喜的場景，輔之以襲擊、俘虜、拯救和脫困等情節。作品為哥德式 (Gothic) 的故事模式，融合血腥駭人的細節。

　　在他的小說裡，角色雖看似平凡，卻能讓人掩卷難忘。小說中的美洲原住民能歸類成兩種：高貴的野蠻人 (the Noble Savages)，如德拉瓦族 (the Delawares) 和摩希根族 (the Mohicans)；而邪惡則如伊洛瓜族 (the Iroquois) 和休倫族 (the Hurons)。原住民在庫柏筆下既是品格高貴的代表，也是哥德式恐怖故事的化身，但皆是新世界殘存的遺民。《最後一個摩希根人》裡的安卡斯，即是站在歷史嬗遞轉折時期的代表，故事暗指美國少數民族面臨滅絕的危險。

　　有學者稱庫柏的《皮襪子故事集》(*Leatherstocking Tales*) 系列和蠻荒小說為美國史詩，因為小說處理美國歷史上的重要議題：西部拓荒、白人與原住民間的衝突等。主角納提・邦波 (Natty Bumppo)，或稱鷹眼，是美國的民族英雄，他也具象了當代人的價值觀：人對蠻荒世界的夢想及憧憬、白人面對原住民矛盾的心態等。

　　庫柏代表一個較古老的美國，描述創建共和國前的地主和紳士貴族階級，思想保守；《皮襪子故事集》可視為對於已經結束的英雄時代和牧歌式田園世界的禮讚和紀念。然而，當今讀者的品味及理念改變，庫柏有些思想恐怕不合時宜——例如奴隸制度有其正當性，或依財產和地位決定投票權等——這些恐怕很難得到現代人的認同，但他的著作仍是瞭解美國思潮的重要來源。庫柏對自然與法律、秩序與改變、蠻荒與文明間的衝突的態度，特別引起現代讀者的省思。

庫柏年表

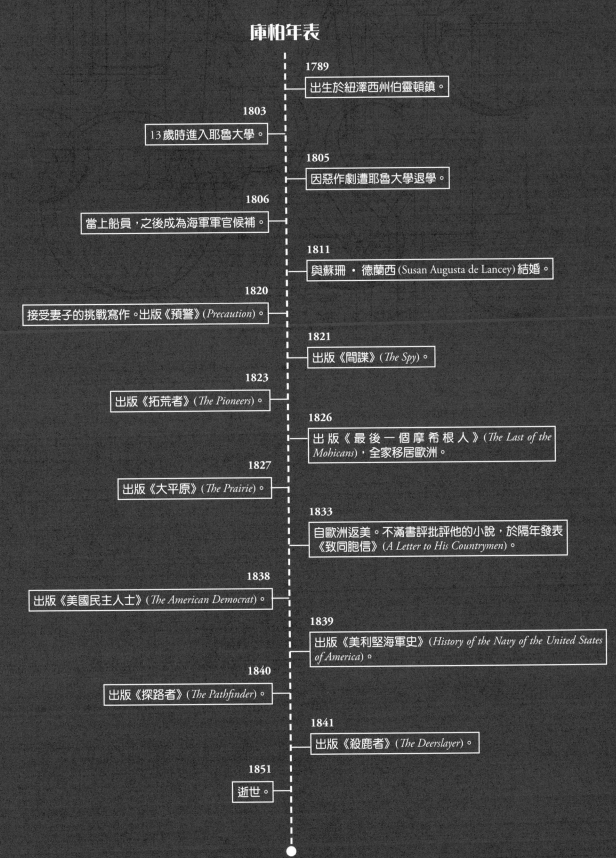

1789
出生於紐澤西州伯靈頓鎮。

1803
13歲時進入耶魯大學。

1805
因惡作劇遭耶魯大學退學。

1806
當上船員，之後成為海軍軍官候補。

1811
與蘇珊‧德蘭西 (Susan Augusta de Lancey) 結婚。

1820
接受妻子的挑戰寫作。出版《預警》(*Precaution*)。

1821
出版《間諜》(*The Spy*)。

1823
出版《拓荒者》(*The Pioneers*)。

1826
出版《最後一個摩希根人》(*The Last of the Mohicans*)，全家移居歐洲。

1827
出版《大平原》(*The Prairie*)。

1833
自歐洲返美。不滿書評批評他的小說，於隔年發表《致同胞信》(*A Letter to His Countrymen*)。

1838
出版《美國民主人士》(*The American Democrat*)。

1839
出版《美利堅海軍史》(*History of the Navy of the United States of America*)。

1840
出版《探路者》(*The Pathfinder*)。

1841
出版《殺鹿者》(*The Deerslayer*)。

1851
逝世。

課文朗讀　完整 Track 2／分段 Track 2-1

The **immense**[1] forest **unfolded**[2] as a dangerous and **untamed**[3] **realm**[4] where humanity*'s impact was small. The dark forest made the battles between distant European nations look unimportant. Indeed, their soldiers were not eager to fight, since the forest unnerved* them.

In 1757, working with several Native American tribes, the French commander Montcalm sent soldiers to take the English **fort**[5] William Henry. Meanwhile, Major Duncan Heyward was leading Cora and Alice to safety at Fort William Henry, where their father Munro was in command. Along the way, David Gamut, a naive Christian*, joined them. They then saw an Indian* named Magua. He offered to guide them to safety, but he led them down the winding paths.

After a while, the group ran into Hawkeye, a scout for the English army, and his Mohican friends, Chingachgook and his son Uncas. Hawkeye didn't trust Magua, suspecting he worked for the French. When they questioned Magua, he ran off. Guessing that Magua would try to attack them later, Hawkeye led the group to a secret cave on an island. The next morning, Magua and some Hurons attacked the group.

They captured Heyward, Gamut, and the Munro sisters. Magua admitted that he sought revenge on Munro. Strangely, he said he would let the group go if Cora would agree to marry him, but she refused. Later, Hawkeye and his friends returned to rescue them. The group continued carefully on their journey to Fort Henry, but they feared

---

Something You Should Know

The mountains looked green, and fresh, and lovely... thin vapors floated between them and the sun. The numerous islands rested on the bosom of the Horican... as if embedded in the waters... among which the fishermen of the beleaguering army peacefully rowed their skiffs, or gloated at rest on the glassy mirror... The scene was at once animated and still. All that pertained to nature was sweet, or simply grand; while those parts which depended on the temper and movements of man, were lively and playful. (*The Last of the Mohicans*, 1826)

　　這是庫柏在小說第 15 章，描寫孟羅 (Munro) 和女兒共處的和諧景象原文摘錄。烘托此景的是窗外的夕陽、遠方蒼綠的山丘、氤氳中的小島，和穿梭在湖上、泛著小舟的漁翁。這個安詳自然的景觀，短暫而溫馨，與之平行的是孟羅家庭團聚的甜蜜場景。庫柏以「漁夫」的意象代表生命，加上「動」與「靜」的對比，暗示人和自然互利共生的關係。庫柏認為自然的規律與人類的生活相似。例如在第 6 章，鷹眼 (Hawkeye) 和秦柯古 (Chingachgook) 在奔往亨利要塞的路上，曾駐足屏息靜觀格蘭斯瀑布 (Glenn's Fall) 的景色。庫柏描述人身體器官的運作，暗喻自然週期亦復如此。清教徒或庫柏同代人將自然視為妖魔，或想像自然一片荒蕪虛空的景象，對比之下，庫柏似乎更關心自然生態環境。

Magua would get more Huron **warriors**[6] to attack them again.

The group moved through the woods at night. When they approached Fort Henry, they saw French soldiers camped nearby. As they came down the mountainside, Alice heard her father shouting commands. She cried out, and the gates of the fort opened to receive them; Cora and Alice were **reunited**[7] with their father.

The French attacked Fort Henry and defeated the English. Heyward then helped Munro surrender to Montcalm, who promised they could leave the fort in peace with their weapons and flags.

The next morning, English men, women, and children began to march peacefully out of the fort. However, as the French stood by, a Huron warrior tried to take a colorful shawl* from one of the women. When she resisted, he killed her and her baby. Magua then urged the Hurons to attack the English, leading to a massacre*. During the **chaos**[8], Magua **kidnapped**[9] Cora and Alice. Gamut secretly followed them.

Words for Production

1. immense [ɪˋmɛns] *adj.* 巨大的；遼闊的
2. unfold [ʌnˋfold] *v.* 展開
3. untamed [ʌnˋtemd] *adj.* 未開發的
4. realm [rɛlm] *n.* [C] 領域
5. fort [fɔrt] *n.* [C] 堡壘
6. warrior [ˋwɔrɪɚ] *n.* [C] 戰士
7. reunite [͵rijuˋnaɪt] *v.* 使重逢
8. chaos [ˋkeɑs] *n.* [U] 混亂
9. kidnap [ˋkɪd͵næp] *v.* 綁架

Words for Recognition

*humanity [hjuˋmænətɪ] *n.* [U] 人性、人類
*unnerve [ʌnˋnɝv] *v.* 使緊張；使不安
*Christian [ˋkrɪstʃən] *n.* [C] 基督徒
*Indian [ˋɪndɪən] *n.* [C] 美洲印第安人 (為舊式且冒犯的說法)
*shawl [ʃɔl] *n.* [C] 披肩
*massacre [ˋmæsəkɚ] *n.* [C] 屠殺

Idioms and Phrases

1. run into 偶然遇見
2. run off 逃跑
3. cry out 大喊

★ ★ ★ Discussion ★ ★ ★

How would you describe Alice and Cora Munro's attempt to make their way to their father? Exciting? Terrifying?

Fort William Henry lay in ruins. Uncas, Chingachgook, Hawkeye, Heyward, and Munro were worried about Cora and Alice. Heyward found their footprints* and guessed Magua had taken them.

The search was difficult. They were careful not to leave footprints in order to avoid Huron warriors. They **paddled**[10] a canoe across a large lake and later began to hike. After forty miles, the group found some human tracks and a recent campfire*. Magua, Cora and Alice were near. That night in the fog, they met Gamut.

Disguised as an Indian, Gamut told them that Cora and Alice were alive—but kept in different places. The Hurons let Gamut walk around freely because they thought he was crazy. Heyward managed to enter the village with Gamut by dressing up as a medicine man. A Huron war party was just arriving at the village with two **captives**[11]; one was the Mohican Uncas.

Heyward spoke secretly to Uncas and began to look for Alice. An Indian asked Heyward, as a medicine man, to cure his mad wife, and Heyward agreed. When Heyward was taken to see the mad woman in a cave, a bear followed him in. In order to trick the Hurons, Heyward began a magic dance to cure her. Then, the bear **growled**[12] and took off his head; it was Hawkeye! Heyward told Hawkeye that Uncas was being held prisoner. Then Hawkeye, still in bear disguise, climbed a tree and saw where Alice was hidden. Heyward then went out to find Alice—and proposed to her. Magua suddenly appeared in the cave and threatened to **torture**[13] Heyward. But, before Magua could get help, the bear squeezed him tightly and Heyward tied him up. Hawkeye then

---

Something You Should Know

美洲的原住民部落 (Native Americans)

　　美洲的原住民部落甚多，散居新大陸各地。庫柏小說裡介紹的原住民，有以下幾族：阿爾岡昆族 (the Algonquins) 是父系部落的原住民，早期定居在聖勞倫斯河與安大略湖東邊。這個族曾經有 50 到 60 個部落。德拉瓦族 (the Delawares)，居住在德拉瓦河流域和德拉瓦港灣區。他們是三個阿爾岡昆族的部落合組的同盟。17 世紀末他們先遭伊洛瓜族 (the Iroquois) 征服，而後土地又被英軍佔領。他們慢慢向西遷居，經由賓州、俄亥俄州、印地安納州，到堪薩斯州與奧克拉荷馬州。他們不以力服人，不擅掠奪和侵略。伊洛瓜族是北美的原住民「六族同盟」而成的聯盟，下又細分許多小集團組合的聯盟。早期大多住在聖勞倫斯河、哈德遜港灣、俄亥俄州南方與肯塔基州。休倫族 (the Hurons)，是母系部落的原住民，住在聖勞倫斯河岸邊。一向與伊洛瓜族不睦，且最早與法軍結盟。在 1649 年的戰役中，他們遭伊洛瓜族擊敗，散居各處。摩希根族 (the Mohicans) 是庫柏合組兩個阿爾岡昆族新創的名字，集馬希根族 (the Mahicans) 和摩黑根族 (the Mohegans) 於一。

led Heyward and Alice out of the cave.

Hawkeye took Alice and Heyward to a friendly Delaware village, and then he returned to the Huron village to rescue Uncas. When Gamut and Hawkeye approached Uncas, Hawkeye gave Gamut a knife and told him to cut Uncas loose. They then traded costumes. Uncas put on the bearskin, Gamut put on Uncas's cap and shirt, and Hawkeye put on Gamut's blanket and hat. Gamut stayed in Uncas' room and pretended to be Uncas. Uncas and Hawkeye left the Huron village and crossed the forest back to the Delaware village.

Words for Production

10. paddle [`pædl] *v.* 用槳划船
11. captive [`kæptɪv] *n.* [C] 俘虜
12. growl [graʊl] *v.* 吼叫
13. torture [`tɔrtʃɚ] *v.* 折磨；使痛苦

Words for Recognition

*footprint [`fʊt͵prɪnt] *n.* [C] 足跡
*campfire [`kæmp͵faɪr] *n.* [C] 營火

Idioms and Phrases

4. in order to 為了

★ ★ ★
Discussion

By far, who do you think is the most important character in this story? Why?

Magua had entered the Delaware village before them and asked the Delawares to give Cora to him. Magua also told them that Uncas was in their village and warned them about Hawkeye being a **notorious**[14] Indian-killer. The Delawares called a village meeting, led by old chief Tamenund. At that moment, Cora, Alice, Heyward, and Hawkeye entered the meeting. Tamenund decided that Magua could leave with his prisoners. Hawkeye and Heyward were then tied up, and Magua could take Alice away.

Tamenund then noticed Uncas' green turtle tattoo* and knew that he was the **descendant**[15] of great warriors. Uncas boldly jumped forward, cut Hawkeye loose, and asked that the prisoners be freed. Tamenund agreed to let Hawkeye, Heyward, and Alice go but decided that Magua could take Cora as his wife. Magua quickly left the Delaware village with Cora.

Now, Chingachgook took command of the group and led them and the Delwares through the forest to fight the Hurons. They defeated the Hurons, but Magua escaped and hid in the cave where he kept Cora. The group followed him in. As they got closer, Magua and two warriors grabbed Cora. They began climbing a steep hill at the other side of the cave.

Cora stopped moving along the narrow ledge* and refused to go farther. Magua threatened to kill her but could not do it. Another Huron then killed Cora. Uncas leaped down to the ledge, screaming and killing the Huron who murdered Cora. Magua then stabbed Uncas in the back and killed him. **Cornered**[16] by Hawkeye, Magua tried to escape by jumping down the mountain, but Hawkeye shot him dead.

The Delawares had defeated the Hurons, and then they **mourned**[17] their dead. Munro, Gamut, and Heyward grieved quietly beside Cora's body. Nearby,

---

Something You Should Know

野蠻與文明世界 (Savagery and Civilization)

　　庫柏利用對比討論原始蠻荒(原住民的生活)與文明開化(白人的責任)。在壯美遼闊的景觀描述中，小說暗示著原住民潛藏的威脅。美國獨立建國前夕，白人不斷地向西拓展，向大自然予取予求，也總是與原住民陷入掠奪土地的衝突裡。故事中，庫柏安排馬瓜(Magua)向柯拉(Cora)求婚被拒，或讓喜歡柯拉的安卡斯(Uncas)遇害，不僅標明異族同婚的困難，也說出原住民(象徵野蠻)在未被教化(象徵文明)之前，種族歧視或階級意識仍是不易跨越的鴻溝。此外，鷹眼拓荒的理念，則隨著時移勢遷，也在故事後半慢慢消失。戰爭最終可能帶來毀滅或死亡，這是貫穿全書的主題；而原住民的土地，他們賴以維生的條件和生命也一一被剝奪。代表進步文明的白人勝利，而象徵蠻荒未開化的原住民黯然退出歷史舞臺。庫柏認為歷史的發展不外乎征服掠取和挫敗逐出，如此的規律無法逆轉。

Chingachgook sat before the body of Uncas.

At Uncas' **funeral**[18], Chingachgook expressed his love and sadness for his son. Hawkeye told him Uncas' spirit would stay by his side. Tamenund declared, "I have lived to see the last warrior of the wise race of the Mohicans!"

The women spoke of the love shared by Cora and Uncas, hoping the lovers would be united in death. Munro said, "The Being we all **worship**[19] will be mindful* of all, without **distinction**[20] of sex, or rank, or color!" Hawkeye replied that people first needed to respect each other. After Cora and Uncas were buried, the Europeans left. Still, it seemed the Native American way of life would disappear.

Words for Production

14. notorious [noˋtorɪəs] *adj.* 惡名昭彰的
15. descendant [dɪˋsɛndənt] *n.* [C] 子孫
16. corner [ˋkɔrnɚ] *v.* 逼到絕境
17. mourn [mɔrn] *v.* 哀悼
18. funeral [ˋfjunərəl] *n.* [C] 喪禮
19. worship [ˋwɝʃɪp] *v.* 崇拜、尊敬
20. distinction [dɪˋstɪŋkʃən] *n.* 差別、不同

Words for Recognition

*tattoo [tæˋtu] *n.* 刺青
*ledge [lɛdʒ] *n.* 自懸壁突出的部分
*mindful [ˋmaɪndfəl] *adj.* 注意的

Idioms and Phrases

5. tie up 牢牢綁緊

★ ★ ★
Discussion

Cooper believed in the idea of progress in society and civilization. Does the novel indicate that he had any doubt on that idea?

一、閱讀測驗 (Reading Comprehension)

(　　) 1. What happened when Hawkeye encountered Magua for the first time?

　　　　(A) Hawkeye thought Magua was a sincere man.

　　　　(B) Hawkeye got into a quarrel with Magua.

　　　　(C) Hawkeye invited Magua to work with him.

　　　　(D) Hawkeye felt that Magua was quite suspicious.

(　　) 2. How did Heyward manage to enter the Huron village?

　　　　(A) He disguised himself as a medicine man.

　　　　(B) He pretended that he had already gone crazy.

　　　　(C) He sneaked into the village in the middle of the night.

　　　　(D) He killed a Huron warrior and put on the victim's clothes.

(　　) 3. How did Tamenund find out that Uncas was the offspring of great warriors?

　　　　(A) He learned the truth from Hawkeye.

　　　　(B) He was shown an ancient document.

　　　　(C) He observed Uncas' green turtle tattoo.

　　　　(D) He noticed the necklace Uncas was wearing.

(　　) 4. Which of the following statements is NOT true?

　　　　(A) Uncas and Cora were actually in love with each other.

　　　　(B) The last of the Mohicans was killed by the French army.

　　　　(C) Hawkeye shot Magua dead when Magua was trying to escape.

　　　　(D) It was Chingachgook that led the Delawares to defeat the Hurons.

二、字彙填充 (Fill in the Blanks)

1. _____ Al Capone, a n_____s gangster, had murdered lots of people before his death.

2. _____ The enemy t_____ed the soldier to obtain some confidential information.

3. _____ The country was in a state of c_____s when the king died unexpectedly.

三、引導式翻譯 (Guided Translation)

1. 昨晚 Michael 在一家義大利餐廳裡偶然遇見他的前女友。

　 Michael _____ _____ his ex-girlfriend in an Italian restaurant last night.

2. 在與 Sean 分別這麼久之後，她一見到 Sean 便激動地喊著他的名字。

　 After being separated from Sean for so long, she _____ _____ his name in excitement as soon as she saw him.

3. 那群強盜將那個有錢人緊緊綁住，並且藏在一個山洞裡。

　 The rich man was _____ _____ and hid in a cave by the bandits.

賞析

這是庫柏五部曲《皮襪子故事集》(*Leatherstocking Tales*) 系列的第二部小說。小說前半部敘述英軍要塞遭受法軍和美洲原住民休倫族人襲擊。後半部描寫白人探子鷹眼,在摩希根族的秦柯古和他兒子安卡斯的協助下,擊退馬瓜為首的休倫族。

故事裡的美洲原住民大致可分成兩類:一類忠誠善良、樂意助人,例如秦柯古和安卡斯;另一類是扮演反面角色的馬瓜等。庫柏在書中摘錄彌爾頓的《失樂園》(*Paradise Lost*) 的詩行,把馬瓜比喻為似撒旦的人物:足智多謀的領袖、口才辯捷無礙,是膽識十足的勇士。當然,他殘忍的屠殺,讓他變成暗黑王子。馬瓜曾在要塞和法軍談判休戰。當時孟羅曾羞辱、鞭打他。庫柏再次引用《失樂園》,暗指孟羅這樣的懲罰的確踰越規紀:他不是上帝,只是一位來自英國帶有種族歧視的白人。庫柏摘錄《威尼斯商人》(*The Merchant of Venice*) 做為引語,暗示馬瓜猶如劇中的猶太商人夏洛克,為了報復種族歧視的言語和侮辱,馬瓜才變成撒旦。但是,報復的結果帶給摩希根人的傷害遠大於孟羅家人。倖存的孟羅哀悼女兒柯拉遇害,而秦柯古卻得面對喪子和滅族的悲痛。

悼念昔日榮耀是貫穿小說標題和敘事結構的主旋律,並以老酋長朗誦輓歌結束全書。白人的貪婪掠奪以及對原住民文化的冷漠不尊重,帶來一連串毀滅性的報復和死亡。暗指遠在美國創建之初,美國的理想和希望早已幻滅,留下的土地一片荒蕪。或許《最後一個摩希根人》形塑的椎心之痛,是庫柏發自內心不安的吶喊:為了成就未來的美國,得殺害一個偉大的民族,毀掉一片遼闊的土地嗎?

庫柏在小說裡還創造一個神話般的人物鷹眼,他的本名叫納提‧邦波 (Natty Bumppo)。他幾乎不受文明的誘惑,而與蠻荒自然維持和諧的關係。或許他是歸化美國的亞當,荒原是他的伊甸園。在《最後一個摩希根人》的結局,他離開文明社會,回到尚未開化的邊區。鷹眼沒有夏娃,只有秦柯古;沒有愛情,卻和摩希根族人成為歃血為盟的弟兄。

在故事中,鷹眼與秦柯古曾在亨利要塞停留。庫柏暗示兩人是離開白人的世界,或以歐陸為中心構建的歷史,走向神話、魔幻和蠱惑巫術的世界。這一系列的首部曲,庫柏即開宗明義道出,法國和美洲原住民間的戰爭起源於為了爭奪土地而衍生出的衝突和矛盾,導致浴血廝殺的悲劇。第二部《最後一個摩希根人》,描寫原住民墜入虛無深淵的開端。戰爭一旦啟動,將無力挽回。白人舉著「進步」的大旗,奪取他們的土地;假「文明教化」之名,剝奪他們原來信奉的傳統儀式。《最後一個摩希根人》除了描述戰爭下的動盪不安、驚心動魄的廝殺和穿插其間的愛情,也同時梳理潛藏故事底層的種族、帝國、環保意識、暴力與建國等議題。

Moby Dick

Herman Melville

關於作者

　　學者稱赫爾曼・梅爾維爾 (Herman Melville, 1819–1891) 為海洋小說家。他有多部作品皆敘說在浩瀚的大海中，人面臨的挑戰和對人性的淬鍊。梅爾維爾從 19 世紀默默無聞到 20 世紀的聲譽鵲起猶如一則傳奇故事。細究之下，因他探討的課題與當代人息息相關。同時代其他作家塑造浪漫情懷的美國神話，語調明亮樂觀；梅爾維爾思考的則是人類「內心世界的掙扎」，描述面對造化的無情及生命的無奈，人總是在善惡、明暗兩端拔河。而梅爾維爾代表的是一種「悲劇的人文主義」，尊重生命但卻浩嘆命運的不公。

　　梅爾維爾出生於殷實的家庭，但之後由於父親早逝，家道中落。他當過雇員，做過莊稼農事、教師，最後當上船員。可能受成長背景影響，他筆下的主角常是歷經文明洗禮，有著開闊胸襟堅持理念的現代人。他在往返利物浦的商船上的工作經驗出現在《瑞德朋》(*Redburn*) 小說中，而後他陸續在航行於南太平洋中的三艘捕鯨船上工作，也在馬克薩斯群島與原住民生活數月，這些經歷融入《泰匹》(*Typee*)，《歐摩》(*Omoo*) 和《白鯨記》(*Moby Dick*) 三部作品。在此同時，他寫了兩部重要的短篇小說：虛無絕望面對生命的《錄事巴托比》("Bartleby, the Scrivener") 與因黑奴叛亂而身心受創的《貝尼托・瑟瑞諾》(*Benito Cereno*)。後期，他在紐約擔任海關檢查員，維持生計，並且開始寫詩，《克拉瑞爾》(*Clarel*) 是一首長達一萬八千行的敘事詩，描述人對聖地的失望和信仰的幻滅。《水手比利巴德》(*Billy Budd, Sailor*) 是梅爾維爾間隔三十年後重回敘事創作的作品，也是他的最後一部小說，處理的同樣是兩難的課題，探討個人的善良與社會法律的公正間的掙扎。

"Both jaws, like enormous shears, bit the craft completely in twain."

—*Page 510.*

▲《白鯨記》1892 年出版品 (C. H. Simonds Company) 的插畫。

　　梅爾維爾受到最多評論和詮釋的是《白鯨記》。書中探討的主題極廣：個人主義、自由平等、人與巨獸對抗、人與海的搏鬥、善惡的拔河、生死的掙扎，到創造與追尋等。梅爾維爾的偉大在於他在貌似平凡的捕鯨事件中探討深層豐富的意義，把紀實的小說當作史詩傳奇來重新構想。最終孜孜深究的是無解的謎團：人面對永遠存在的善與惡之間的拔河。

梅爾維爾年表

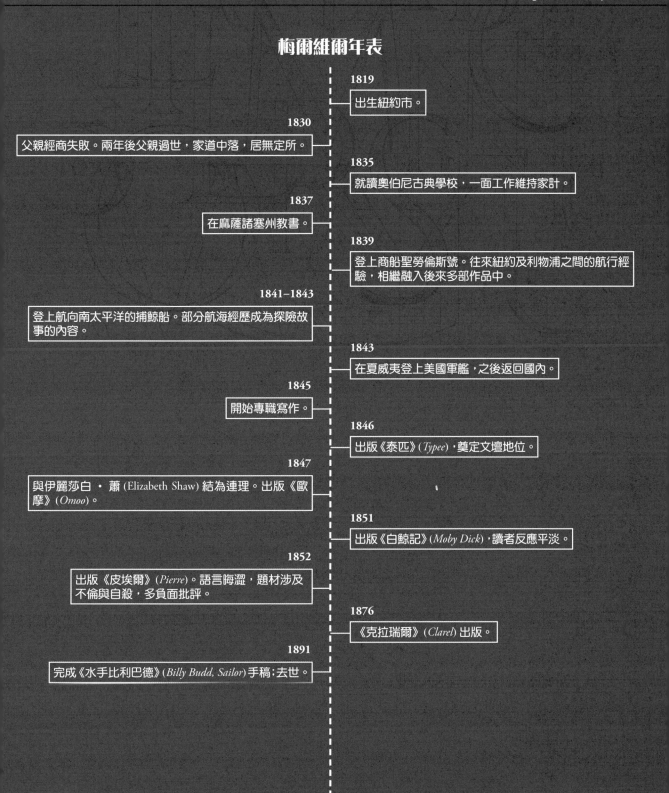

1819

出生紐約市。

1830

父親經商失敗。兩年後父親過世,家道中落,居無定所。

1835

就讀奧伯尼古典學校,一面工作維持家計。

1837

在麻薩諸塞州教書。

1839

登上商船聖勞倫斯號。往來紐約及利物浦之間的航行經驗,相繼融入後來多部作品中。

1841–1843

登上航向南太平洋的捕鯨船。部分航海經歷成為探險故事的內容。

1843

在夏威夷登上美國軍艦,之後返回國內。

1845

開始專職寫作。

1846

出版《泰匹》(*Typee*),奠定文壇地位。

1847

與伊麗莎白 · 蕭 (Elizabeth Shaw) 結為連理。出版《歐摩》(*Omoo*)。

1851

出版《白鯨記》(*Moby Dick*),讀者反應平淡。

1852

出版《皮埃爾》(*Pierre*)。語言晦澀,題材涉及不倫與自殺,多負面批評。

1876

《克拉瑞爾》(*Clarel*) 出版。

1891

完成《水手比利巴德》(*Billy Budd, Sailor*) 手稿;去世。

課文朗讀　完整 Track 3／分段 Track 3-1

For days, the *Pequod* had been at sea, sailing south across the Atlantic Ocean, and the whaling ship's mysterious captain was yet to show his face to the crew. Ahab was his name and to most of the crew, all that was known of him was only a rumor that he was a grand ungodly god-like man. He was a man of few words but of deep meaning who had both attended colleges and lived among **savages**[1]. He was an expert whaler* who had lost his leg, hunting the great white sperm whale*, known to all as Moby Dick.

And then one morning, the sound of his false leg on deck marked Ahab's first appearance to the men. A long white **scar**[2] ran down the side of his face and he wore a false leg made entirely out of a whale's jaw bone. With a **grim**[3] expression, he was a frightening man who, through both fear and **awe**[4], commanded the **utmost**[5] respect from the men under him.

As the ship traveled further south, closer to the waters of the whales, Ahab spent less and less time in his quarters, becoming increasingly restless. To the **disquiet**[6] of his crew, he would often pace back and forth across the deck during the late hours of the night with the noise of his false leg passing through the ship to the crew quarters below.

Then, one day, Ahab **assembled**[7] the whole crew around him and began a speech.

"What do you do when you see a whale, men?" he asked.

"Sing out for him!" they replied.

Then he asked, "And what do you do next, men?"

"Lower away, and after him!" they shouted.

Something You Should Know

On the starboard hand of every woe, there is a sure delight; and higher the top of that delight, than the bottom of the woe is deep... Delight—top-gallant delight is to him, who acknowledges no law or lord, but the Lord his God, and is only a patriot to heaven... I have striven to be Thine, more than to be this world's, or mine own. Yet this is nothing; I leave eternity to Thee; for what is man that he should live out the lifetime of his God? (*Moby Dick*, 1851)

　　以上的摘錄是「匹科德號」出發前，梅坡神父在教堂發表的一篇證道詞，其中他引申《聖經》原文：「上帝已準備了一條大魚去吞沒約拿。」而在這段證道詞的末尾是這樣說的：在每一場苦難背後，都必定有一種欣喜，這種欣喜遠高過痛苦之深……願堅信上帝者、在臨終時能感謝天父的人會有永世的愉快及甜美。我已力爭想獲得上帝的庇佑，遠超過想立足於這世界或忠於自我的慾望，但這都是微不足道的事。我將永生留給上帝，因何人能比上帝活得更久？

　　這段證道詞可視為《白鯨記》故事的縮影或亞哈悲劇的開場白：亞哈不向律法或爵爺低頭，只向上帝低頭，只承認他自己是法律。而他把本應只屬於上帝的權力掌握在他自己手中，這從他痛恨「莫比‧迪克」必欲除之才甘心的態度得到佐證。

"And what tune is it do you all live by, men?"

"A dead whale or a **smashed**[8] boat!" they cried excitedly.

With the crew acting as one and of the same mind, Ahab began to talk of the white whale. To the first sailor to spot the whale, he would offer a Spanish gold coin as reward. His true intentions were made clear. Effortlessly, he persuaded them to abandon their mission of gathering whale oil, and instead, hunting the cause of Ahab's injury, the great white terror, Moby Dick. Now the crew were with him in his chase for revenge, except one.

"Why seek revenge on a dumb **brute**[9] that attacked you out of blindest instinct!" cried Starbuck, the ship's first mate.

"I would strike the sun if it insulted me," Ahab responded.

Overpowered by Ahab's charisma*, the crew were swayed. They celebrated throughout the night, drinking to the death of Moby Dick. The next day, they determined to hunt the white whale.

Words for Production

1. savage [`sævɪdʒ] *n.* [C] 野蠻人
2. scar [skɑr] *n.* [C] 傷疤，傷痕
3. grim [grɪm] *adj.* 嚴肅的；冷酷的
4. awe [ɔ] *n.* [U] 敬畏；驚嘆
5. utmost [`ʌtmost] *adj.* 最大 (限度) 的
6. disquiet [dɪs`kwaɪət] *n.* 擔心；不安
7. assemble [ə`sɛmbl̩] *v.* 集合
8. smash [smæʃ] *v.* 猛烈撞擊；打碎
9. brute [brut] *n.* [C] 野獸

Words for Recognition

*whaler [`hwelɚ] *n.* [C] 捕鯨人
*sperm whale [`spɝm‚hwel] *n.* 抹香鯨
*charisma [kə`rɪzmə] *n.* 個人魅力；號召力

Idioms and Phrases

1. back and forth 來回
2. out of 出於

★★★ Discussion

Describe Ahab's physical appearance and discuss how this adds to the impression of the character.

One quiet night, one seaman, while working in the **rear**[10] of the ship, heard a strange sound coming from a part of the ship no crew member was allowed to go. It was not the first, nor the last time of the strange noises were heard to come from there. One day, the lookout* on the mast* spotted a herd of sperm whales. "There she blows!" he shouted. The crew sprang into action, lowering the whale boats to take up the chase. A strange group of men emerged from the depths of the ship. None of them had been seen before. The mystery of the unusual sounds coming from the forbidden section of the ship was explained. They were Ahab's personal harpoon* crew that he had **snuck**[11] aboard the night before the *Pequod* set sail. Five harpoon crews—**manning**[12] five whale boats—were on the hunt. One of them was commanded by Ahab himself despite both his **disability**[13] and the fact that captains rarely left the ship to go on the hunt. The harpooner on Starbuck's boat, Queequeg, landed a harpoon on one of the whales, but the beast turned the boat over and managed to escape. The hunt was unsuccessful.

The *Pequod* sailed southeast, rounding the southern coast of Africa. Often at night, a silver spout* was seen in the distance which appeared to be the blowout* of a whale's breath. But no matter how hard they tried, they could never catch up with it. Some of the men claimed it to be Moby Dick himself, making fun of them as if trying to trick

---

Something You Should Know

透視《白鯨記》創作的年代

　　首先，那是一個美國民族情緒昂揚樂觀的時期。自 1776 年獨立建國到 1812 年與大英帝國的第二次戰爭獲勝，全國瀰漫著希望，向外拓展的信念強烈。梅爾維爾是少數洞悉明亮陽光下隱藏著危機的作家，《白鯨記》揭露了生命中暗藏的恐怖和無法理解的悲劇。

　　其次，那是一個擴張的時代。特別是 1849 年加州淘金潮的推波助瀾，更是助長了拓荒精神。但在此階段，也造成了堪薩斯州和內布拉斯加州邊界的戰爭。或許，匹科德號代表的正是那種橫渡七海五洋，到處獵捕魚獲，無役不與的拓展精神。但是在征服大海的表相下，卻也暗藏許多邪惡和醜陋。

　　第三，那是一個宣揚極端個人主義的世代。美國以擺脫宗教和政治的枷鎖，獨立建國自詡。因此鼓勵個人向外拓荒、自力更生，這種特性可說是化外「粗獷的個人主義」(rugged individualism) 精神，猶如生活在蠻荒原始的世界，得暫卸下文明教化的包袱，出自本能的展現勇氣與膽識，劈荊斬棘、開疆闢土。若將亞哈船長放在愛默生的「自立」(self-reliance) 的信念檢視美國精神，他其實是一個極端且帶有悲劇性的例子。

　　最後，那是一個鼓勵勤奮積極的年代。精進淬煉自我的能力，闊步努力向前是美國移民的精神。個人付出的心血，聚沙成塔，可以完成更大的任務。捕鯨船就是一個社會的縮影，需要個人捨棄專斷蠻橫的自我，協力為共同的目標和利益努力。缺乏人性關懷而一味追求目標，終非美國立國的精神。

them into following him. Northeast they sailed, ever watchful for any signs of the white whale. Along the way they met other whaling ships, but Ahab would only gather with them if they knew anything about where Moby Dick was.

Ahab continued to hunt other whales to keep the crew busy. He did not want them to think about whether or not it was worthy to pursue the white whale for no other reason than to satisfy a captain's **ego**[14] and his control over them. They caught two whales without any incident and went about processing them as whalers do, harvesting them for their oil.

As they sailed further east, signs of Moby Dick's presence and influence increased. They came across an English ship, the *Samuel Enderby*, whose captain had lost one of his arms to the whale. Further on, after entering the Pacific Ocean, they came into contact with the *Rachel*, whose captain had lost his son after an encounter with Moby Dick. And then, at a gathering with another ship, the *Delight*, Ahab learned that they had passed a smashed whale boat where four seamen had lost their lives to the whale. As the *Pequod* sailed further on, an encounter with that white sperm whale was meant to happen.

Words for Production

10. rear [rɪr] *n.* 後面
11. sneak [snik] *v.* 偷偷地走;溜
12. man [mæn] *v.* 在⋯崗位上工作;操縱
13. disability [ˌdɪsəˈbɪlətɪ] *n.* [C] [U] 殘障
14. ego [ˈigo] *n.* 自尊心;自負

Words for Recognition

*lookout [ˈlʊkˌaʊt] *n.* [C] 瞭望員
*mast [mæst] *n.* [C] 船桅,桅杆
*harpoon [hɑrpun] *n.* [C] 捕鯨叉
*spout [spaʊt] *n.* 噴水;噴出
*blowout [ˈbloˌaʊt] *n.* [C] 噴出

Idioms and Phrases

3. set sail 啟航
4. catch up with 趕上
5. make fun of 嘲笑

★ ★ ★ Discussion

Why does Ahab want to kill the white whale? What do you think about it? Is it reasonable or foolish?

One night, Ahab suddenly caught the **scent**[15] of a whale. Moby Dick was near. At dawn, he climbed up the main mast. He was nearly two thirds up the mast when he at last spotted the white whale a mile away. "There she blows!—there she blows! A hump* like a snow-hill! It is Moby Dick!" Ahab had earned his own reward, the Spanish gold coin. After a year at sea, the hunt for Moby Dick had begun. The harpoon boats were lowered and they set off in pursuit. However, soon after, the whale dove down into the depths of the ocean and disappeared from their sight. At first, Ahab saw nothing. Then peering down into the ocean, he glimpsed a small white spot. Gradually, the white spot grew and it was not long before it became huge. There was no doubt that it was Moby Dick and it was heading directly for Ahab's boat. Ahab tried to **steer**[16] the boat away, but it was too late and the beast crushed the boat in two between its huge jaws. Fortunately, the *Pequod* arrived just in time to scare the whale off before it could kill Ahab and the rest of his harpoon crew.

The next day, the hunt was on again. Despite what happened the day **prior**[17], Ahab was more than ever intent on taking the whale down. Moby Dick was sighted and the crew, inspired by Ahab's determination, followed Ahab into danger again. Fearlessly, Ahab attacked the whale head-on*, sticking it with many harpoons. The whale responded by striking one of the boats that then crashed with another, **disabling**[18] them both. Ahab's boat was the only one remained. He and his crew were almost killed by the mass of rope and harpoons that moved violently as the whale struggled about in

---

Something You Should Know

It was a black and hooded head; and hanging there in the midst of so intense a calm, it seemed the Sphynx's in the desert. "Speak, thou vast and venerable head," muttered Ahab, "which, though ungarnished with a beard, yet here and there lookest hoary with mosses; speak, mighty head, and tell us the secret thing that is in thee. Of all divers, thou hast dived the deepest. That head upon which the upper sun now gleams, has moved amid this world's foundations. Where unrecorded names and navies rust, and untold hopes and anchors rot..." (*Moby Dick*, 1851)

　　白鯨或莫比・迪克，到底代表什麼？小說中有不同的解釋。有人說牠是不會講話的野獸；亞哈則說牠是「深潛海洋中的大怪魔」，是大自然中不服從人類且與人敵對的元素；有的水手則將牠當作上帝的化身。梅爾維爾在書中，編織所有的經典神話，賦予莫比・迪克神秘的特質和力量。海上的捕鯨人相信牠是不朽且無所不在的。讀者也許可以說白鯨是匯聚宇宙的驚異、詭譎、玄妙、美麗及恐怖於一。牠善惡黑白兼備，人欲探索其終極的意義，何其困難。猶如人難尋生命的真諦，因為生命始終曖昧不明，撲朔迷離。

the water. Ahab's boat was turned over and he lost his false leg in the process. Defeated again, he barely managed to escape back to the *Pequod* with his life.

"He's chasing me now; not I, him—that's bad," Ahab exclaimed. Ahab finally realized that Moby Dick would be the end of him, but he resolved to kill him, or die trying. On the third day, the whale was spotted again. Ahab, **yielding**[19] to his fate, again entered his boat. The whale surfaced beneath the other two boats, damaging them both and quickly going under the surface again. Reemerging, Moby Dick headed directly for the *Pequod* itself, smashing it with his huge head. The ship sank. As a last desperate attempt, Ahab speared* the whale before he was dragged down to the sea depths by a flying rope that caught him around the neck. As for the rest of the crew, they were drawn down by the strong currents created by the sinking *Pequod*. Only one man survived to tell the tale of Moby Dick. His name was Ishmael, the narrator of this story. In his arrogance, Ahab had **defiantly**[20] challenged the forces of nature, but lost.

Words for Production

15. scent [sɛnt] *n.* 野獸的氣味；獸跡
16. steer [stɪr] *v.* 駕駛；掌方向盤
17. prior [`praɪɚ] *adj.* 在前的
18. disable [dɪs`ebl̩] *v.* 使喪失能力；使失靈
19. yield [jild] *v.* 屈服
20. defiantly [dɪ`faɪəntlɪ] *adv.* 挑戰地；傲慢地

Words for Recognition

*hump [hʌmp] *n.* [C] 隆起，凸起
*head-on [`hɛd`ɑn] *adv.* 迎頭相撞地
*spear [spɪr] *v.* 用魚叉刺

Idioms and Phrases

6. at last 最後
7. as for 至於

★ ★ ★
Discussion

How would you describe the giant white whale and the relationship between marine creatures and humans at that time?

一、閱讀測驗 (Reading Comprehension)

(　　) 1. Which of the following statements regarding Ahab is NOT true?

    (A) He lost one of his legs to a giant white whale.

    (B) He chose to become a sailor instead of going to college.

    (C) He seldom spoke, but he was a great and capable leader.

    (D) There was a long white scar on the side of his face.

(　　) 2. Why were there strange noises coming from the forbidden part of the *Pequod*?

    (A) The captain's personal crew were hidden there.

    (B) A few cats were chasing large rats on the ship.

    (C) A giant whale was trying to attack and ruin the ship.

    (D) There were some terrible ghosts haunting the ship.

(　　) 3. At that time, what was the common and main reason for hunting whales?

    (A) To sell their meat to the rich.

    (B) To eat their internal organs.

    (C) To kill them simply for fun.

    (D) To obtain the oil from them.

(　　) 4. According to this story, which of the following statements is TRUE?

    (A) Ahab successfully took revenge on Moby Dick in the end.

    (B) Moby Dick tried its best to ruin *Pequod* but did not succeed.

    (C) The story of Moby Dick was told by Ishmael, the only survivor.

    (D) Ahab hated Moby Dick because it had slaughtered his family.

二、字彙填充 (Fill in the Blanks)

1. _____ Being late, Emma tried to s_____k in the classroom quietly but was caught by the teacher right away.

2. _____ The principal a_____ed all the students and then delivered a speech.

3. _____ Mom looked very g_____m and didn't say anything after knowing that I failed both my math and chemistry exams.

三、引導式翻譯 (Guided Translation)

1. 船長確認全員登船後才啟航前往目的地。

The captain made sure everyone was on board before he _____ _____ for the destination.

2. 出於好奇心，那個男孩打開了他在閣樓發現的那個木箱子。

_____ _____ curiosity, the boy opened the wooden box he had found in the attic.

3. 當 Vicky 聽到同學因 Greg 臉上胎記而戲弄他時，她告訴他們這很沒禮貌。

When Vicky heard other classmates _____ _____ _____ Greg because of his birth mark on the face, she told them it is rude.

賞析

　　《白鯨記》是部以史詩形式描繪海洋的小說。梅爾維爾敘述捕鯨的故事及藝術，並且提供讀者豐富詳實的鯨魚類種和相關知識。

　　人對海洋的認識有限，謙卑以對，理應能與萬物和諧相處。人對鯨魚也是略識之無，若以開放的態度接納，假以時日，同樣能掀開牠神祕生態的面紗。《白鯨記》以辯證的模式推移，時而採戲劇形式呈現，時而用敘述紀實演繹，不停地探索恆久縈繞人心的哲學和宗教。船長亞哈的行動貌似單純，卻充滿戲劇張力：他因大腿遭鯨魚截斷，執意追捕報復，將白鯨當作邪惡的化身。此外，《白鯨記》裡也使用了許多不同的技巧，包括第一人稱的敘事者(故事透過以實瑪利敘述)、劇場上的舞臺指令(例如「後甲板」和「午夜／水手艙」章)、戲劇獨白(從「日落」到「初夜班」章)、內在或心理的自剖(「日落」章)、目錄排比(「鯨類學」)、故事中的故事(「巨鯨出水的故事」)、無所不知的敘事者技巧(每當以實瑪利無法詳加解說，或情節語調改變時，就會出現全知觀點的敘事者來說故事)，或是利用倒敘情節或回憶等。

　　《白鯨記》也可看作禮讚海洋的史詩。在描述陸地的章節裡，海洋的意象已隨處可見。梅爾維爾呈現自燠熱赤道到嚴寒海角南端的各類型氣候帶的風貌，海洋從寧靜平和到瘋狂暴烈的形象，兼而有之。如描述一船員初次擔任桅頂瞭望班時，他的心思被浪潮與思潮的混和韻律，催眠得六神無主。但他同時也臆想「腳底下神祕的海洋，猶如擁有深邃、湛藍、無涯靈魂的魔力，滲透在人與自然之間」。他相信大海擁有浩然之氣，能開啟人恢弘的視野。梅爾維爾認為大海也是試煉英雄氣質的場域：身處神祕、危險和孤寂的環境裡，人得持續追尋探索。人在極其困頓絕望、永無止息的戰鬥中，愈能突顯傲然獨立、不屈不撓的靈魂本質。

　　《白鯨記》或梅爾維爾的其他作品，處理的內容與現代人關心的課題極其相似：宇宙是否存在亙古不變的規律和秩序？人們唯一可以確信的是：在規律的宇宙週期中，生命仍有難解的神祕。若生命的意義可以用色調來比喻，梅爾維爾呈現的世界確如其書中對白鯨的描述：虛無空白。一言以蔽之，白鯨抑或大海，乃是集美麗、力量、冒險和無懼之大成，是一則造化宇宙無法解開的謎。亞哈拋棄理性中道，挑戰善變難掌握的命運，率性執意復仇，終以毀滅告終。畢竟，人探索自然或大海終極真相的能力有限，人要有智慧明白如何與世界相處而非對抗。

關於作者

　　納撒尼爾‧霍桑 (Nathaniel Hawthorne, 1804–1864) 出生於麻薩諸塞州的賽勒姆鎮。他的祖先皆是捍衛清教徒正統信仰的教徒，其中約翰‧霍桑 (John Hathorne) 在 1692 年是賽勒姆鎮女巫審判 (Salem Witch Trials) 的法官。納撒尼爾‧霍桑在《紅字》(*The Scarlet Letter*) 的前文〈海關〉("The Custom-House") 中說明自己彷彿受到雙重詛咒，他除了繼承祖先的罪惡，也因為他是藝術家，勢必不會受到清教徒的認可，而成了被詛咒的人。霍桑將他和家族間不安惶惑的關係與裂痕，訴諸筆端化為複雜曖昧、多重疊層的藝術作品。

　　霍桑的作品不下百餘篇；他稱自己寫的是「傳奇」而非小說。他利用寓言和象徵來詮釋真實及超自然的世界，或衝破兩個世界的藩籬，眾多敘述點到為止，讀者彷若置身夢境。他的四大名著《紅字》、《七角閣樓》(*The House of the Seven Gables*)、《歡樂谷傳奇》(*The Blithedale Romance*) 和《大理石牧神》(*The Marble Faun*) 皆是著名的傳奇。他以超然客觀的角度呈現人物和場景，結構完整、修辭細膩、語言凝鍊簡約。他在有限的主題與典型人物裡，處理錯綜複雜的道德與倫理議題。霍桑擅用修辭技巧，避開說教，彰顯真理。

　　霍桑認為昔日歷史必在當今社會烙下深刻的印記，因此他在新英格蘭清教徒思想中尋找題材，相信原罪與邪惡，如同良善，是人性無法割捨的部分。人若無意驅除邪惡或刻意將之隱藏，內心的罪惡終將腐蝕且摧毀人的靈魂。此外，霍桑認為人若脅迫別人屈從你的意志，即是入侵別人神聖的靈魂。這種人犯下的是「不可饒恕的罪」(the unpardonable sin)，是為暗黑的勢力、魔鬼的代理人。相關主題和敘事的技巧在霍桑的故事和傳奇裡不斷出現。如〈年輕善人布朗〉("Young Goodman Brown") 及〈胎記〉("The Birthmark")。

　　霍桑研究並創造道德與心理戲劇張力十足的故事。十七世紀的新英格蘭的生活，表面看來純淨並與世隔離，其實，他們的生活環境艱困，還備受清教徒嚴苛教義的壓迫。霍桑明瞭罪惡是普遍的經驗，無法逃避。他的作品呈現面對魔鬼的誘惑時幽微難測的人性。

霍桑年表

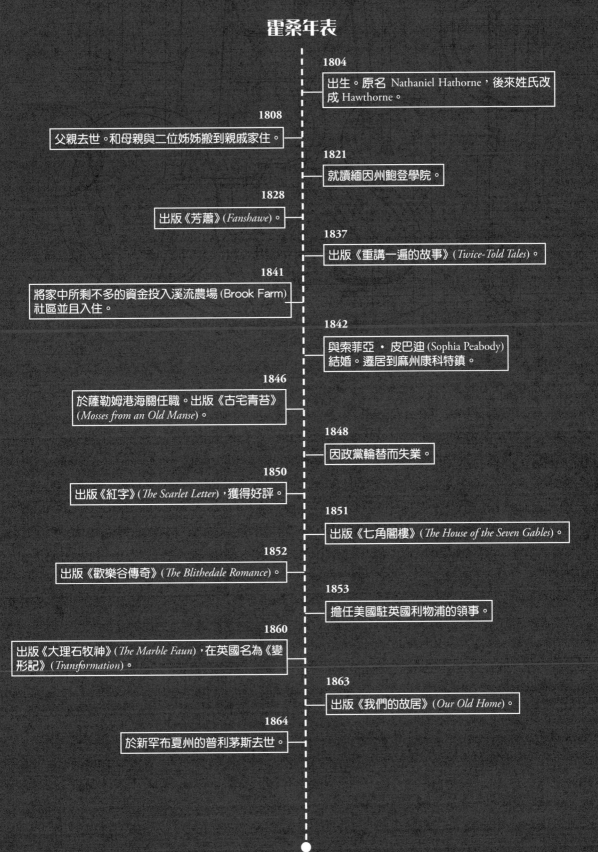

1804
出生。原名 Nathaniel Hathorne，後來姓氏改成 Hawthorne。

1808
父親去世。和母親與二位姊姊搬到親戚家住。

1821
就讀緬因州鮑登學院。

1828
出版《芳蕭》(*Fanshawe*)。

1837
出版《重講一遍的故事》(*Twice-Told Tales*)。

1841
將家中所剩不多的資金投入溪流農場 (Brook Farm) 社區並且入住。

1842
與索菲亞・皮巴迪 (Sophia Peabody) 結婚。遷居到麻州康科特鎮。

1846
於薩勒姆港海關任職。出版《古宅青苔》(*Mosses from an Old Manse*)。

1848
因政黨輪替而失業。

1850
出版《紅字》(*The Scarlet Letter*)，獲得好評。

1851
出版《七角閣樓》(*The House of the Seven Gables*)。

1852
出版《歡樂谷傳奇》(*The Blithedale Romance*)。

1853
擔任美國駐英國利物浦的領事。

1860
出版《大理石牧神》(*The Marble Faun*)，在英國名為《變形記》(*Transformation*)。

1863
出版《我們的故居》(*Our Old Home*)。

1864
於新罕布夏州的普利茅斯去世。

In the mid-1800s, there was a utopian* community called Blithedale Farm. A young poet named Miles Coverdale had decided to live there. Before doing so, Coverdale had gone to see a show featuring the **Veiled**[1] Lady. Hypnotized* by a magician in the show, Coverdale felt that this mysterious woman had special powers to **predict**[2] the future. After the show, he **encountered**[3] an elderly man known as Old Moodie. Moodie asked Coverdale if he knew a woman named Zenobia, but Coverdale replied that he did not.

On a cold April day, Coverdale and his friends traveled to Blithedale Farm. Upon arriving at the farm, they were greeted by a woman named Zenobia, who was wearing a flower in her hair. Coverdale was immediately taken by her beauty. Blithedale Farm was founded on the principles of **mutual**[4] aid, love, and sharing. Unlike the modern selfish and **competitive**[5] society of that time, Blithedale Farm was meant to be a "modern Arcadia*," where people could return to a simple and natural life, work hard together, and make an honest living from the land.

The members of the Blithedale Farm community normally prepared and ate meals together. Their dinner that night, however, was interrupted by the arrival of Coverdale's old friend Hollingsworth, who was accompanied by a pale young girl. This **frail**[6] girl immediately took a liking to Zenobia, but Zenobia did not return the girl's affection. Eventually, the girl revealed that her name was Priscilla.

Unfortunately, Coverdale fell sick, and he had to spend the next few weeks resting. Once Coverdale had recovered, he joined the rest of the group as they worked on the farm. Coverdale noticed that Priscilla seemed to look healthier. He also noticed that Hollingsworth spent a lot of time with Zenobia and Priscilla. In fact, some people

---

Something You Should Know

傳奇 (Romance)

　　霍桑許多的故事皆屬於「傳奇」類型。在美國文學裡，傳奇指的是作家運用虛構的手法處理真實的歷史事件。傳奇最早雖起源於中古世紀，但十九世紀美國文學傳奇的發展，乃回溯至英國華特・史考特 (Walter Scott, 1771–1832) 的歷史傳奇，接著更促成美國寫實小說的崛起。傳奇因時空的異動也愈趨複雜。例如，傳奇到了愛倫坡 (Edgar Allan Poe)、霍桑和梅爾維爾手中成了挖掘內心世界和審視靈魂的形式，虛構、現實或歷史的關係常被拆解，重新檢驗。霍桑曾經在《七角閣樓》(The House of the Seven Gables) 的序言中，簡要說明傳奇與小說的分歧：作家若宣稱自己的作品是「傳奇」，意味著他在形式風格和取材上，擁有特定揮灑的空間；而寫小說則沒有這種特權。撰寫小說重視細節，描寫旨在盡可能準確，或至少貼近事實真相或人生經驗。「傳奇」在某種層次而言，是作者憑藉自己的選擇或創作，表達特定環境下的真相。

in the community had already begun to gossip about Hollingsworth and Zenobia, saying that they appeared to be a couple. Unexpectedly, Moodie turned up at Blithedale and stated that he was Priscilla's father. He was also very interested in how Zenobia had been treating Priscilla. He seemed relieved to find out that Zenobia had been nice to her.

Some time later, Coverdale had gone out on a long walk away from the farm. He encountered a man named Professor Westervelt in the woods. Westervelt repeatedly asked about Zenobia and Priscilla. Later, when Coverdale was at "the hermitage*," a place he went to for **solitude**[7], he was surprised to see Westervelt talking to Zenobia. He eavesdropped* on their conversation, which seemed to indicate that they had had a relationship in the past. Westervelt was also heard saying that Zenobia should do something about Priscilla.

Words for Production

1. veiled [veld] *adj.* 蒙上面紗的
2. predict [prɪ`dɪkt] *v.* 預言
3. encounter [ɪn`kaʊntɚ] *v.* 遇到
4. mutual [`mjutʃʊəl] *adj.* 相互的
5. competitive [kəm`pɛtətɪv] *adj.* 競爭的
6. frail [frel] *adj.* 脆弱的
7. solitude [`sɑlə,tjud] *n.* [U] 獨處

Words for Recognition

*utopian [ju`topɪən] *adj.* 烏托邦的，理想國的
*hypnotize [`hɪpnətaɪz] *v.* 催眠
*Arcadia [ɑr`kedɪə] *n.* 阿爾卡迪亞 (用來比喻牧歌式樂園)；桃花源
*hermitage [`hɝmɪtɪdʒ] *n.* [C] 修道院
*eavesdrop [`ivzdrɑp] *v.* 偷聽

Idioms and Phrases

1. take a liking to . . . 喜歡
2. turn up (出乎意料地) 出現

★ ★ ★
Discussion

What motivates people like Coverdale or Hollingsworth to live in Blithedale Farm? To seek an ideal life, to fulfill a noble cause or...?

課文朗讀 分段 Track 4-2

One evening, Zenobia entertained the group by telling them a story called "The Silvery Veil." In the story, a young man is determined to **uncover**[8] the mystery of the Veiled Lady. He managed to lift her veil, but she disappeared. The story turned to a young lady in the countryside. She encountered a magician in the forest, who claimed that she was in peril. She could be saved only by casting a veil over her new friend, who was once the magician's prisoner. Upon finding her friend, the young lady followed the magician's instruction. The magician then appeared and took the Veiled Lady away. When Zenobia reached this part of the story, she threw some fabric that looked like a veil to Priscilla, leaving her **terrified**[9].

Despite this unusual behavior toward Priscilla, Zenobia often joined Priscilla, Coverdale, and Hollingsworth at a place called Eliot's Pulpit*. There, they engaged in all sorts of debates. Zenobia, for example, was passionate about feminism*. So, Coverdale was very surprised when Zenobia sided with Hollingsworth during a debate, even after Hollingsworth made misogynistic* remarks. What's more, Priscilla, who sat on the ground at Hollingsworth's feet, also agreed with them both. Unfortunately, Coverdale continued to disagree with those around him, especially Hollingsworth. Hollingsworth seemed interested only in using Blithedale Farm for his own cause of **reforming**[10] sinners. The two argued so intensely that Coverdale left Blithedale Farm.

Coverdale returned to Boston. From his hotel room, he could **peek**[11] into the rooms of the building across from the hotel. He was very surprised one day when he looked

---

Something You Should Know

命名與意涵

　　柯伏道 (Miles Coverdale) 不是單純闖入歡樂谷的朝聖客或體驗生活的旁觀者，霍桑的命名另有象徵用意。歷史中的柯伏道 (Myles Coverdale) 出生於 1488 年，在 1535 年他是將《聖經》完整地譯成英語的第一人，而被視為清教徒的領袖。霍桑的柯伏道沒有如此顯赫的成就。《歡樂谷傳奇》裡，柯伏道常觀察大千世界的反面，書中呈現不少對他的負面描述及窺伺的意象。吉諾碧雅投河自盡後，柯伏道找到她的一隻鞋，洗盡汙泥，懸在他屋內做為紀念。

　　故事為何安排吉諾碧雅 (Zenobia) 自殺，這和歷史典故有關。吉諾碧雅是敘利亞帕米拉王國 (Palmyrene Empire, 267–273) 的女王，性格果敢獨立，與故事中吉諾碧雅頗相似。西元 273 年，女王在領導革命，欲自羅馬帝國獨立時慘遭擄獲，據說在移送回國途中自殺。關於吉諾碧雅的原形，後世常認是瑪格麗特・福勒 (Margaret Fuller, 1810–1850)，知名女權人士。她在此作出版的前兩年因船難逝世。福勒、霍桑與愛默生 (Ralph Waldo Emerson) 因溪流農場而有交集。愛默生在悼念文中說她學識豐富、才氣縱橫；到了霍桑的小說裡她卻多了一層神秘的面紗。

over and saw none other than Westervelt with Zenobia and Priscilla in the same room. He watched them, until he was discovered. Zenobia angrily lowered the curtain. Upset, Coverdale raced to their room. Zenobia answered the door and let Coverdale in. As they talked, it dawned on Coverdale that Zenobia was in love with Hollingsworth. Priscilla then appeared, but Zenobia quickly stated that they had another appointment, and the three of them left.

Coverdale was confused. He sought Old Moodie out for answers. Moodie seemed to know more about the girls than anyone else. Coverdale bought Moodie a drink in an attempt to reveal more information. Moodie told a long story about his past. He said that he had once been known as Fauntleroy. When he was rich, he was married and had a daughter—Zenobia. However, he had lost his fortune and his first family and lived in poverty. Later, he remarried and had another daughter—Priscilla, who had a gift for supernatural **perception**[12]. Moodie stated that Priscilla looked up to Zenobia and wanted to be just like her. Moodie also shared that Zenobia's wealth had been **inherited**[13] from Moodie's brother. Moodie, in fact, should have inherited this money, but he had given up this right under the condition that Zenobia promised to treat Priscilla well.

Words for Production

8. uncover [ʌn`kʌvɚ] *v.* 揭露
9. terrified [`terəfaɪd] *adj.* 恐懼的
10. reform [rɪ`fɔrm] *v.* 改革
11. peek [pik] *v.* 窺視
12. perception [pɚ`sɛpʃən] *n.* 感知能力
13. inherit [ɪn`herɪt] *v.* 繼承

Words for Recognition

*pulpit [`pʊlpɪt] *n.* [C] (教堂的) 講壇
*feminism [`fɛmənɪzəm] *n.* 女性主義
*misogynistic [mɪ`sɑdʒənɪstɪk] *adj.* 厭惡女性的

Idioms and Phrases

3. none other than sb /sth 正是… ，竟然是…
4. dawn on sb 使…意識到

★ ★ ★
Discussion

How do you describe the male characters like Coverdale, Hollingsworth or Westervelt and female characters like Zenobia or Priscilla in the story? A list of adjectives may help you: indifferent, sensitive, self-centered, passionate, morose.

課文朗讀 分段 Track 4-3

Coverdale was shocked when Moodie revealed this information. He decided to go to see a show of the Veiled Lady. At the performance, he was surprised to see Westervelt onstage as a magician who seemed to control the Veiled Lady. Coverdale wondered where Priscilla was, but he quickly found out when Hollingsworth climbed up on the stage and called out for Priscilla. Removing the veil, Hollingsworth revealed that Priscilla was the Veiled Lady. Hollingsworth then **escorted**[14] Priscilla off the stage, rescuing her from Westervelt.

Coverdale eventually made his way back to Blithedale Farm. However, as he approached the farm, feelings of unease and anxiety grew inside of him. He wandered around the farm and the woods until he came to Eliot's Pulpit. There, he found Hollingsworth, Zenobia, and Priscilla. They were surprised to see him. Coverdale noticed that Hollingsworth and Zenobia no longer seemed close. Breaking down in tears, Zenobia accused Hollingsworth of being in love with Priscilla, who she now **acknowledged**[15] as her sister. She also claimed that Hollingsworth had only loved Priscilla when Zenobia had lost her fortune to Priscilla, a result of her betraying Moodie and turning Priscilla over to Westervelt. For Priscilla's part, she decided to go off with Hollingsworth, leaving Zenobia alone with Coverdale.

Zenobia **collapsed**[16] to the ground. Desperately, she reached out to Coverdale and begged him to tell Hollingsworth that he was the one who had "murdered" her. **Wailing**[17], Zenobia left and never returned. **Overwhelmed**[18] by emotions, Coverdale found a place to sleep for a few hours, but he was awakened by a bad feeling. He asked if anyone had seen Zenobia. She had not returned to the farm. A search party was

---

Something You Should Know
. . . .

瑪格麗特・福勒 (Margaret Fuller) 與女性意識

　　學者皆認為《歡樂谷傳奇》裡的女主角吉諾碧雅是霍桑同時代的作家瑪格麗特・福勒的化身。福勒是美國超驗主義 (Transcendentalism) 運動的重要一員，也是超驗主義主要刊物《日晷》(The Dial) 的首位編輯。她生前致力於教育改革，她出版的作品，包括捍衛女權的信念，皆顯現她敏捷的才思與高瞻的視野。她追隨女性主義先驅瑪莉・沃斯登葵夫特 (Mary Wollstonecraft) 的腳步，一生宣揚婦女平等。《十九世紀的婦女》(Woman in the Nineteenth Century) 是她的重要著作，透過許多例證闡述女人與男人均應被視為獨立且平等的個體。她接著到歐洲和義大利旅遊，並且投入義大利的民族獨立運動。1850 年返回美國，因船難逝於紐約長島外海。她的著作基本的觀點如下：她鼓勵女人必須仰賴自己，或相互扶持，才能改變自己的生活或命運。她特別指出超驗主義者若堅持廢除奴隸制度，照道理也應該堅持拆除男人加在女人身上的枷鎖。

organized. Hollingsworth, Coverdale, and others eventually found Zenobia's body in the river, where she had killed herself.

A simple funeral was arranged for Zenobia, and she was buried on a hill near Blithedale Farm. Unexpectedly, Westervelt appeared at the funeral, saying that it had been foolish of Zenobia to kill herself because of love. Coverdale disagreed with Westervelt publically, though inside, he actually agreed with him. Zenobia's death had been a waste. He then looked over and saw Priscilla, who seemed to be still completely in love with Hollingsworth.

Years later, Coverdale happened to visit Hollingsworth and Priscilla. Though the two were still together, Hollingsworth had given up on his cause, and he seemed to be **haunted**[19] by the death of Zenobia. As for Priscilla, she was quiet, but protective of Hollingsworth. In her own way, she seemed happy in this role as guardian of the "powerfully built" but now powerless man. Coverdale himself had remained unmarried. He was unhappy; he finally revealed that he had been in love with Priscilla all along.

Words for Production

14. escort [`ɛskɔrt] *v.* 護送
15. acknowledge [ək`nɑlɪdʒ] *v.* 承認
16. collapse [kə`læps] *v.* 崩潰
17. wail [wel] *v.* 慟哭
18. overwhelm [ˌovɚ`hwɛlm] *v.* (在精神上、感情上) 打擊；使困惑
19. haunt [hɔnt] *v.* 縈繞於心

Idioms and Phrases

5. find out 得知
6. no longer 不再
7. break down 痛哭

★ ★ ★
Discussion

What do you think about Zenobia's death and Priscilla's survival? How do their acts affect the male characters in the story?

一、閱讀測驗 (Reading Comprehension)

( ) 1. Which is NOT one of the principles on which Blithedale Farm was founded?
     (A) Love.   (B) Sharing.
     (C) Self-help.   (D) Mutual aid.

( ) 2. Why did Coverdale leave Blithedale Farm and return to Boston?
     (A) He had intense arguments with Hollingsworth.
     (B) He found out that Zenobia didn't love him at all.
     (C) His belief contradicted Blithedale Farm's principles.
     (D) Professor Westervelt disliked him and drove him away.

( ) 3. Which of the following statements regarding Moodie, Zenobia, and Priscilla is NOT true?
     (A) Both Zenobia and Priscilla were Moodie's daughters.
     (B) Zenobia inherited a large fortune from Moodie's brother.
     (C) Priscilla looked up to Zenobia and longed to be like her.
     (D) Moodie had a brother, Fauntleroy, who was very wealthy.

( ) 4. Which of the following statements is TRUE?
     (A) Westervelt refused to show up at Zenobia's funeral.
     (B) Coverdale actually had been in love with Priscilla all along.
     (C) Hollingsworth brutally murdered Zenobia as a form of revenge.
     (D) Priscilla remained single after she broke up with Hollingsworth.

二、字彙填充 (Fill in the Blanks)

1. _____ Amy c_____ed after learning that both of her parents had passed away in the car accident.
2. _____ Charlie felt t_____d when he noticed a stranger was following him.
3. _____ The activist has devoted his life to r_____ming the social system for the poor.

三、引導式翻譯 (Guided Translation)

1. 經理突然出現在會議上嚇到了大家，因為大家都以為她休假去了。
The manager _____ _____ at the meeting and shocked everyone, for everyone thought she was on vacation.

2. 演唱會上，觀眾很驚訝特別來賓竟然是流行搖滾歌手，紅粉佳人。
At the concert, the audience was amazed that the special guest was _____ _____ Pink, the pop rock singer.

3. 當 Phil 看到信用卡帳單時，他才意識到自己最近真的花太多錢了。
When Phil saw credit card bills, it _____ _____ him that he did spend too much money recently.

　　霍桑的《歡樂谷傳奇》帶有部分自傳的色彩，其中包括他自己在超驗主義「溪流農場」(Brook Farm) 生活數月的親身體驗。成員各自懷抱不同的思想來到此社區，嘗試以進步的理想為本，構建一個烏托邦式的理想生活模式 (a Utopian living)。其中一位標杆型的人物，是與霍桑同時代的瑪格麗特‧福勒 (Margaret Fuller)：她一生捍衛女性權利，在故事中以吉諾碧雅 (Zenobia) 之名出現。

　　《歡樂谷傳奇》承襲「溪流農場」的模式，意圖回到烏托邦式純真的伊甸園，或田園牧歌式恬淡淳樸的生活。但是，這則傳奇說明：回到烏托邦世界是純然虛妄的念頭，各主要人物皆各自禁錮於自我困頓的生活中，無法回到純真的世界。普莉斯希拉 (Priscilla) 的經歷即代表：歡樂谷看似一處庇護所，但是，它卻無法保護她免於受到狡詐的偉思特佛教授 (Professor Westervelt) 的威嚇。

　　歡樂谷社區成員們各自的性格削弱了實現理想的機會。柯伏道 (Coverdale) 任性輕佻、憤世嫉俗；何林沃斯 (Hollingsworth) 則固執己見、執意教化犯人；吉諾碧雅具傲氣、耽於感官享受，最後證明熱情反是摧毀她的力量。何林沃斯成了三角戀情的主角，不但毀了吉諾碧雅，也斷送了他自己和普莉斯希拉的一生。

　　這部傳奇之所以成為霍桑的重要作品，關鍵在他創造柯伏道這個人物。柯伏道體現縈繞在霍桑想像世界的典型人物：冷漠矜持，超然孤立，與世人永遠保持距離。柯伏道總是假裝事不關己的態度，但卻喜歡窺伺別人的行動。他不想真心經營自己的感情 (例如，他極力掩飾或壓抑他其實很喜歡普莉斯希拉)，卻耽溺於偷聽別人在談情說愛時的密語或窺視朋友的行為，他覺得愧疚，暗示自己心理有問題。違背人類心靈的神聖，在霍桑眼中是極重大的罪惡。霍桑擔心藝術家總是保持冷漠、超然觀察者的立場，在現實生活尋覓貼切的美學形式呈現，但卻忘記自己也生活在滾滾紅塵，理應抱有悲憫同情的心看待世人。

　　吉諾碧雅原先捍衛婦女權利的理想，卻因仰慕男權至上的何林沃斯而失去動力。原先憂鬱寡歡的普莉斯希拉，最後也成了失去方向、漫無目標的象徵。但是，故事到最終，有人自殺 (吉諾碧雅)，有人身心屬弱 (何林沃斯)，有人失去活下去的動力 (柯伏道)，脆弱的普莉斯希拉彷彿是故事中唯一的倖存者。

　　《歡樂谷傳奇》全書以「普莉斯希拉！」之名結束，恰如其分。她具體呈現時代的毫無生機和撲朔迷離的現實，也正反映霍桑對當時社會道德的混亂和文化的分崩離析的感嘆。

關於作者

馬克・吐溫 (Mark Twain, 1835–1910)，原名山姆・蘭亨・克萊門 (Samuel Langhorne Clemens)，是繼承美國寫實主義傳統的作家。馬克・吐溫是他的筆名，原意河道「二尋深」(two fathoms deep)，是密西西比河上的船舶能安全通航的深度。他的文字融入本土的幽默和地域特色鮮明的風格，奠定他在美國文學史上的重要地位。

作品呈現的幽默和諷刺來自不同的源頭，大致可分成三大類。第一類是美國新英格蘭的傳統，馬克・吐溫運用婉約含蓄的形式，批判人物的墨守常規。第二類是以描述動物行為、人物誇張的表現、言過其實的情節，或以框架小說 (frame story) 敘述等方式呈現。第三類是西方文學的喜劇傳統。馬克・吐溫把故事寫得逸趣橫生，因為他懂得融入文學的訣竅，例如穿插粗俗的諷刺、荒誕的用語或錯誤的引證等。《頑童歷險記》(*The Adventures of Huckleberry Finn*) 裡的兩個騙子滑稽地表現《哈姆雷特》裡著名的獨白，即充分表現馬克・吐溫反諷的技巧。

馬克・吐溫的作品有明確批判的目標。他嘲諷的事物包括君主體制、改革運動、哥德尖拱式的建築，或濫情華麗的敘述等，這一切皆和浪漫主義有關。他排斥浮誇地表達感情，堅持寫實直白地描述。

簡單介紹幾部重要作品一窺他的文學成就。《湯姆歷險記》(*The Adventures of Tom Sawyer*) 描述一位富有幻想的孩童，行事總是戲劇化。其中馬克・吐溫對墓園、鬼屋、小島和洞穴情景的描繪，從平凡到高潮，添加神祕傳奇的元素。個別人物刻畫細膩，例如小鎮醉漢、法官的假髮或校長的迂腐。而《頑童歷險記》的主題甚多，其中「自我」與社會的衝突最引人深思。主角哈克尋找不受文明拘束，不受傳統限制的生活。比起陸上的暴力、殘忍和腐敗，哈克認為河和邊界象徵逃避、自由與安全，也是他嚮往的去處。馬克・吐溫生命的後期曾有些波折，面對黯淡的歲月，「自我」成了他覓得寧靜平安的方寸之地。也許《頑童歷險記》裡對哈克的撰述是他對文學的禮讚，他相信憑藉藝術和文字的想像可以創造新天地，衝破黑暗綻放光芒。他為後人創造了許多難忘的人物和引人深思的生命課題。

吐溫年表

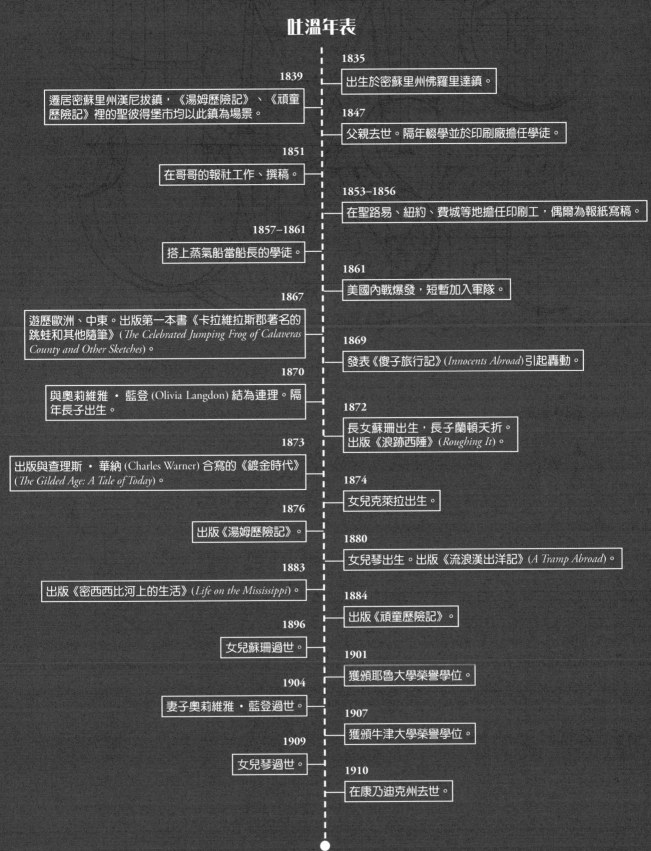

1835
出生於密蘇里州佛羅里達鎮。

1839
遷居密蘇里州漢尼拔鎮，《湯姆歷險記》、《頑童歷險記》裡的聖彼得堡市均以此鎮為場景。

1847
父親去世。隔年輟學並於印刷廠擔任學徒。

1851
在哥哥的報社工作、撰稿。

1853–1856
在聖路易、紐約、費城等地擔任印刷工，偶爾為報紙寫稿。

1857–1861
搭上蒸氣船當船長的學徒。

1861
美國內戰爆發，短暫加入軍隊。

1867
遊歷歐洲、中東。出版第一本書《卡拉維拉斯郡著名的跳蛙和其他隨筆》(*The Celebrated Jumping Frog of Calaveras County and Other Sketches*)。

1869
發表《傻子旅行記》(*Innocents Abroad*)引起轟動。

1870
與奧莉維雅・藍登 (Olivia Langdon) 結為連理。隔年長子出生。

1872
長女蘇珊出生，長子蘭頓夭折。
出版《浪跡西陲》(*Roughing It*)。

1873
出版與查理斯・華納 (Charles Warner) 合寫的《鍍金時代》(*The Gilded Age: A Tale of Today*)。

1874
女兒克萊拉出生。

1876
出版《湯姆歷險記》。

1880
女兒琴出生。出版《流浪漢出洋記》(*A Tramp Abroad*)。

1883
出版《密西西比河上的生活》(*Life on the Mississippi*)。

1884
出版《頑童歷險記》。

1896
女兒蘇珊過世。

1901
獲頒耶魯大學榮譽學位。

1904
妻子奧莉維雅・藍登過世。

1907
獲頒牛津大學榮譽學位。

1909
女兒琴過世。

1910
在康乃迪克州去世。

With his friend, Tom Sawyer, Huckleberry Finn found a robber's stash of gold and got rich overnight. Unable to find his father, the bank held the gold he had found in trust, and put Huck into **Widow**[1] Douglas' care. Huck Finn was not happy living with Widow Douglas and her sister, Miss Watson. Coming from a low-class background, Huck Finn was uneducated and his new guardians attempted to **civilize**[2] him. He became frustrated with his new life of cleanliness, manners, school, and church. However, in order for Huck to take part in Tom's new "robbers' gang," Tom requested him to be "respectable." Therefore, he tried his best to live the proper life that his new guardians required of him. Huck hated the rules Miss Watson made him follow and the religious beliefs she **imposed**[3] on him, but he coped with her overbearing* nature by keeping his opinions to himself. Aside from getting up to mischief here and there with Tom and the rest of the robbers' gang, Huck settled into a routine of home and school. Even though he preferred his old life, he began to enjoy some of his new life, too.

All was well until his abusive* father's return. A drunk and a **bully**[4], Pap Finn demanded to have Huck's money. Concerned for his well-being, the Widow attempted to gain full custody* of Huck, but the judge ruled against it. His father, who hadn't changed at all, continually harassed him around town. After being told to stay away from Huck by the Widow, Pap became so angry that he kidnapped his son and kept him in an **isolated**[5] cabin across the river. Whenever Pap went out, he locked Huck up in the cabin, coming home drunk and occasionally beating him. The beatings became more frequent and severe, and Huck decided he needed to leave.

One day, after finding an abandoned canoe, Huck came up with a simple, yet

---

Something You Should Know

密西西比河的象徵意義

　　密西西比河在《頑童歷險記》包涵多層的意義。首先，水在神話中與生命、創造息息相關，象徵誕生及復活。哈克幾次從岸上消失，象徵他的死亡 (如第 7 章，假裝自己遭謀殺)；當他從河上返回陸地，常以偽裝或新的身分出現 (第 11 章，偽裝成女孩；第 32 章，冒充自己是湯姆)。

　　此外，對照腐敗殘忍的陸地生活 (第 17 與 18 章，葛蘭福德家和薛普德生家的宿怨和謀殺)，這條河代表寧靜、自由和安全。在葛薛兩姓家族血鬥後，哈克歌頌大河恩賜他們自由及木筏給他們自在安靜的生活。

　　水還有宗教的意義：經歷河水的洗禮，人可以象徵性的滌除汙垢、洗淨罪惡。哈克和吉姆隨著密西西比河向前旅行，每一轉折，都會遇到險境。但這條河總能將他們帶出險境，導向另一個不確定的嘗試，繼續追求自由。

clever plan. He couldn't simply just leave or else his father would never stop looking for him, so he planned to fake his own death. He killed a pig and spread its blood all over the cabin to make it look like the work of robbers. Then, he traveled downstream and hid on an island in the middle of the Mississippi River, watching the townspeople look for his body. After living on the island for a few days, Huck encountered Jim, one of Miss Watson's slaves. Jim had fled after learning he was going to be sold to a **plantation**[6] downriver where he would be treated badly. Huck decided not to give Jim up, and instead followed his own moral **intuition**[7] and kept Jim's secret. They teamed up and lived a simple and peaceful life on the island.

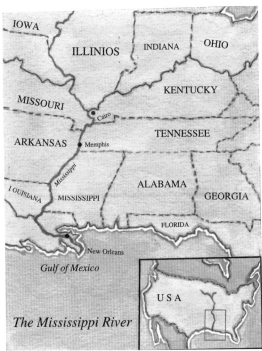

▲密西西比河流域。

Words for Production

1. widow [ˋwɪdoʊ] *n.* [C] 寡婦
2. civilize [ˋsɪvḷˌaɪz] *v.* 使文明；使有教養
3. impose [ɪmˋpoz] *v.* 強制實行
4. bully [ˋbʊlɪ] *n.* [C] 仗勢欺人者
5. isolated [ˋaɪsḷˌetɪd] *adj.* 孤立的
6. plantation [plænˋteʃən] *n.* [C] 種植地；農園
7. intuition [ˌɪntuˋɪʃən] *n.* [C] [U] 直覺

Words for Recognition

*overbearing [ˌovɚˋbɛrɪŋ] *adj.* 專橫的
*abusive [əˋbjusɪv] *adj.* 辱罵的
*custody [ˋkʌstədɪ] *n.* [U] 監護；照管

Idioms and Phrases

1. take part in sth 參加 (某事)
2. get up to sth 忙於；從事
3. come up with 想出
4. or else 否則

★★★ Discussion ★★★

What do you think is the principal function of the river in this story?

課文朗讀 分段 Track 5-2

One day, the river flooded and the two spotted a **raft**[8] and a house floating past their island. They acquired the raft, looted the house and came across a **corpse**[9] of a man who had been shot. To protect Huck, Jim prevented him from seeing the dead man's face. Unfortunately, the pair was forced to leave the island after Huck learned that there was a reward for Jim's capture and that people were planning to search the island for him. Taking the raft and the canoe, the two headed downriver. They planned to float to Cairo, where they would sell the raft and then take a steamboat* up the Ohio River to the free states where **slavery**[10] was forbidden. As they were approaching Cairo, Jim told of his plans to save every penny he earned towards buying his wife and children back from the slave owner. He even **proclaimed**[11] that he would go so far as to steal them if the slave owner refused to sell them.

One night, as they were on their way to Cairo, a thick fog settled and the two became separated. Huck and Jim spent the night looking for each other. Eventually, Huck found Jim sleeping on the raft and decided to play a prank* on him. He pretended that they hadn't been separated at all and that he had just been sleeping. Jim became confused and upset and argued with Huck about the events of the previous night. Jim realized Huck had been playing tricks on him and told Huck how worried he was for

---

Something You Should Know

I would do the right thing and the clean thing, and go and write to that nigger's owner and tell where he was; but deep down in me I knowed it was lie—and He knowed it. You can't pray a lie—I found that out... But I didn't do it straight off... And got to thinking over our trip down the river; and I see Jim before me, all the time... I couldn't seem to strike no places to harden me against him, but only the other kind... and then I happened to look around, and see that paper... I was a-trembling, because I'd got to decide, forever, betwixt two things, and I knowed it. I studied a minute... and then says to myself: "All right, then, I'll GO to hell"—and tore it up. It was awful thoughts, and awful words, but they was said; and never thought no more about reforming. (The Adventures of Huckleberry Finn, 1884)

馬克‧吐溫對人類社會彼此殘忍相向的態度頗有微詞，因此，他把希望的光芒投射在哈克的身上。從以上摘錄可見哈克決定放棄他那個時代的社會價值觀 (白人把黑奴當作家產，及擁有支配黑奴的一切權利)。相反的，哈克把吉姆當作人類同胞看待。他做此決定，全憑自己的良心；或許他還年輕，沒有足夠的智力決定一切，也不可能把同情心用到整個黑人種族上。但是，即使只用在吉姆身上，對哈克如此年輕的孩子來說，實為一大進步。他面對頑強的傳統社會與宗教的壓力，仍能訴諸自己的良知，平等待人，忠於吉姆，寧願自己「入地獄」也不肯出賣朋友，實在難能可貴。

Huck when they became separated and how relieved he felt when he woke up to find Huck was safe. After seeing Jim's reaction to Huck's prank, Huck began to consider the feelings of his companion. Feeling guilty for tricking Jim, Huck decided to humble himself to Jim by apologizing.

Jim became increasingly excited and anxious as he got closer to freedom while Huck began to experience a crisis of conscience. Feeling bad about helping what he understood as someone else's property, he decided to turn Jim in. While on the canoe, looking to see if they had reached Cairo, Huck encountered a band of slave hunters. However, he couldn't bring himself to give Jim up to them, even when he learned about the value of the reward for capturing Jim. Huck covered for Jim by telling the slave hunters that Jim was his father suffering from smallpox*. Fearing for their lives, the hunters left them alone. Later, they realized they had already passed Cairo in the fog. Their plan to row back upstream was stopped in its tracks when they woke to find their canoe had been stolen. Their bad luck continued when, the next night, a steamboat **collided**[12] with their raft and the pair was separated.

Words for Production

8. raft [ræft] *n.* [C] 木筏
9. corpse [kɔrps] *n.* [C] 屍體
10. slavery [slevərɪ] *n.* [U] 奴隸制
11. proclaim [proˋklem] *v.* 宣佈；聲明
12. collide [kəˋlaɪd] *v.* 相撞

Words for Recognition

*steamboat [ˋstimˌbot] *n.* [C] 汽船
*prank [præŋk] *n.* [C] 玩笑；惡作劇
*smallpox [ˋsmɔlˌpɑks] *n.* [U] 天花

Idioms and Phrases

5. go so far as to . . . 甚至；竟然

★★★ Discussion

Choose an episode in the story and share your thoughts on Huck's personality.

課文朗讀 分段 Track 5-3

Huck ended up as a guest of a wealthy family, the Grangerfords, who owned a large **estate**[13] near where Huck and Jim were separated. Huck enjoyed his time there among the generous family, **befriending**[14] a Grangerford boy named Buck, but things soon began to get worse. The Grangerfords were in the middle of a long and bitter feud* with another family, the Shepherdsons, the cause of which no one could remember. The fighting between them **escalated**[15] when a Grangerford girl ran off with a Shepherdson boy. Led by a Grangerford slave, Huck was reunited with Jim. While Huck was returning from his reunion with Jim back to the estate, he witnessed the pointless killings of two young Grangerfords, one of whom was Buck. Huck decided to return to Jim and the raft and leave the troubles behind him. Both of them decided that the peace of the river life was best for them.

However, their peaceful life was short-lived. They were joined by two con men* who they had rescued from **bandits**[16]. The men got up to all sorts of troubles, first by tricking a small village into watching their fake performances and then by pretending to be the long-lost uncles of some orphan girls. Deciding that his dishonest companions were **immoral**[17], Huck told the girls of the con men's **deception**[18] and attempted to help them. Later, the whole town got involved in the affair. Huck got away and back to the raft, hoping to get rid of the con men. Unfortunately, the con men followed soon after and Huck and Jim were forced to travel with their unwanted companions.

As a final act of wickedness, the con men sold Jim back into slavery. Huck, with

---

Something You Should Know

I am rotten glad of it, because if I'd a knowed what a trouble it was to make a book I wouldn't a tackled it and ain't a-going to no more. But I reckon I got to light out for the Territory ahead of the rest, because Aunt Sally she's going to adopt me and sivilize me, and I can't stand it. I been there before. (*The Adventures of Huckleberry Finn*, 1884)

這段摘錄是哈克故事結束時，向讀者道別的一段話。故事開始時，哈克追求自由，因為他必須逃避華特生小姐的「文明」，以及避免自己隨時可能死在父親手中的危險。原先旅行的動機十分單純：帶著「離開一切」的心境，幫助吉姆逃到自由地區。然而，經歷河上和陸地的各種困難和考驗後，如今，哈克又要回家了，但他覺得自己已無家可歸 (父親已死)，也不想要莎莉姑媽「收養、教化他」。哈克原先只是一名社會的棄兒；現在，他卻成了道德的孤兒，因為他無法接受傳統的道德觀，而恰好這又是「文明」的一部分。特別在旅途中，他目睹許多文明社會展現的醜陋：偽善的宗教、殘酷的家族械鬥、對奴隸的冷漠，或凶惡的暴民等。因此，他只好準備再度動身上路。哈克追求的自由雖然難以捉摸，但他仍以羨慕的口吻，描述自己和吉姆徜徉在密西西比河那種寧靜安詳的自由。

the help of Tom Sawyer, who he had recently met up with, resolved to set him free.

Even though the plan worked, Tom was shot in the process and Jim, instead of running away, decided to stay with him while Huck looked for a doctor. When Tom recovered from a fever, he realized the adventure was over and it was time for him to tell everybody the truth that he had been hiding: Jim was already free. Miss Watson, Jim's former owner, had died a few months earlier and Jim's freedom had been mentioned in her will. Jim later also revealed to Huck that the dead man they encountered in the floating house was, in fact, Huck's father, Pap. After all his experiences with the people on his adventures, Huck came to the conclusion that he didn't want to be civilized. Huck's escape from his father and society was to seek freedom and a new life. The **inhumanity**[19] of the feud and **fraud**[20] he met prompted Huck to appreciate more the idyllic* life of peace and brotherhood he and Jim had experienced. He later recognized and treated Jim as his equal human being.

Words for Production

13. estate [ɪˋsteɪt] *n.* [C] 大片私有土地；莊園
14. befriend [bɪˋfrɛnd] *v.* 做朋友
15. escalate [ˋɛskəleɪt] *v.* 惡化；加劇
16. bandit [ˋbændɪt] *n.* 土匪；盜賊
17. immoral [ɪˋmɔrəl] *adj.* 道德敗壞的
18. deception [dɪˋsɛpʃən] *n.* [C][U] 欺騙
19. inhumanity [ˏɪnhjuˋmænətɪ] *n.* [U] 不近人情，殘酷
20. fraud [frɔd] *n.* [U] 欺騙

Words for Recognition

*feud [fjud] *n.* [C] (特指兩人、兩個家族、兩個民族間長期的) 不和，宿怨
*con man [ˋkɑnˏmæn] *n.* [C] 騙子
^idyllic [aɪˋdɪlɪk] *adj.* 田園詩的，牧歌的

Idioms and Phrases

6. end up 最後變成⋯
7. get rid of 擺脫

★★★ Discussion

Compare the personalities of Huck and Jim. How do they differ or resemble?

一、閱讀測驗 (Reading Comprehension)

( ) 1. After Huck faked his own death, where did he hide?

    (A) In a cabin located deep in the forest.

    (B) On an island in the middle of a river.

    (C) In a basement of an abandoned house.

    (D) On an old and broken ship at the beach.

( ) 2. Which of the following statements about Jim is TRUE?

    (A) Huck had been friends with him in Miss Watson's house.

    (B) He wanted to buy his parents and children back.

    (C) He fled because his master often beat him badly.

    (D) His former owner gave him freedom before she died.

( ) 3. Why did Huck decide to leave the Grangerfords?

    (A) He didn't want to get involved in the fight between the two families.

    (B) He thought that the members of the Grangerfords looked down on him.

    (C) He missed Widow Douglas so much that he wanted to reunite with her.

    (D) His father came and threatened to kill him if he didn't leave the Grangerfords.

( ) 4. What's the identity of the dead man Huck and Jim ran across in the floating house?

    (A) Tom Sawyer.

    (B) An evil bandit.

    (C) Huck's father.

    (D) Buck Grangerford.

二、字彙填充 (Fill in the Blanks)

1. _____ Mary just b_____ded a handsome guy from Italy on the Internet.

2. _____ The newly elected mayor p_____med that he would do his best to crack down on crime in the city.

3. _____ The notorious b_____y was finally expelled from the school.

三、引導式翻譯 (Guided Translation)

1. Tom 想出一個能說服媽媽買新電動玩具給他的計畫。

Tom _____ _____ _____ a plan to persuade his mom to buy him the brand new video games.

2. Julia 不喜歡壁紙的顏色，所以很樂意擺脫它。

Julia didn't like the color of the wallpaper, so she'll be happy to _____ _____ _____ it.

3. 我們必須在八點前吃完晚餐，否則我們會來不及搭上最後一班公車回家。

We need to finish dinner before eight o'clock, _____ _____ we won't be able to take the last bus home.

賞析

　　這是一部描述少年成長的小說。哈克嚮往自由，想要擺脫羈絆，但一路上他歷經各種試煉道德準則的考驗：吉姆是脫逃的黑奴，站在白人的立場，哈克不應眼睜睜看著吉姆逃走。他擬好一封給華特生小姐的信，表示只要拿到賞金，就會交出吉姆。哈克後來卻開始猶豫，想起吉姆對他的照顧頓時讓他覺得良心不安。他實在找不到可以狠心對付吉姆的理由，哈克終於決定「好吧，我下地獄去好了」。然後，他把寫好的信撕掉。故事暗喻孩童天生的美德與智慧遠勝過所有現實世界既定的原則。

　　哈克是個秉性純良的孩子，沒有受到文明或教育的腐化。他常以稚童天真的眼睛，記錄現象，分辨虛實。他的反應總帶有同理心與人情味，並憑良知做出決定。例如，是否該把吉姆送回做奴隸，及當他目擊薛普德生家族槍殺葛蘭福德家族的孩子後，他打從心裡厭惡這種暴力的行為，他的反應都是直接訴諸本能的。哈克的反應再次揭發了所謂文明社會的虛偽和殘忍：兩個家族的宿怨，可以在禮拜天上教堂，聆聽牧師傳播福音，講兄弟之愛、善行及神恩浩蕩時，仇恨暫時得到紓解。但是走出教堂，卻可因嫌隙，射殺無辜孩子洩恨。或許這可以解釋為何哈克在小說最後宣布他要往西部邊疆去，不想讓莎莉姑媽收留他，學做文明人。表面上哈克似乎不願接受家庭教育，其實故事的結尾點出了全書的主旨：接受文明的洗禮豈非就是接受或默許暴力、殘忍和虛偽的存在？如果是這樣，他寧願回到純樸的自然中。

　　吉姆在哈克的成長過程中扮演多重角色。在順著密西西比河的旅程中，吉姆取代哈克父親的位置，教導哈克如何適應環境，因地制宜的生活；而且他還像母親呵護孩子一般，付出他無私的愛和犧牲，甚至最後為了救湯姆，冒著被送回做奴隸的危險。這些舉動再再證明吉姆善良的品格和發自內心的人性光輝。相對於陸地上遇到的狡猾騙子、偽善的人物，或殘殺無辜之人的行為，哈克在吉姆身上看到許多高貴的品德。有趣的是，吉姆和哈克皆屬於社會的邊緣人：前者是脫逃的奴隸，後者為了躲避父親而逃離。兩人象徵性從岸上世人的眼中消失，代表他們昔日的自我死亡，但是歷經密西西比河的洗禮，他們找回新的生命和新的自我。

　　這是一部描述少年持續不懈地想實現自己嚮往的目標，在遭欺壓時仍努力付出，追求自由的故事。貧窮的白人孩子想躲避家暴，非裔美國人則想掙脫奴役的枷鎖。雖然出生背景不同，兩人堅持信念，克服困難。礙於階級、年齡和膚色，文明社會總是帶著愚昧、偏見與殘暴的態度，把他們視為次等人。然而，他們卻在各自的身上找到希望、勇氣和高尚的品德。

"Paul's Case: A Study in Temperament[1]"

關於作者

薇拉 · 凱瑟 (Willa Cather, 1873–1947) 雖出生在美國東岸，卻是在中西部的內布拉斯加州長大。1895年大學畢業後，即在不同的報刊雜誌擔任編輯和專欄作家。她在 1903 年《四月的曙光》(*April Twilights*) 詩集出版後，陸續有《巨人花園》(*The Troll Garden*)、《噢，拓荒者！》(*O Pioneers!*)、《我的安東妮亞》(*My Ántonia*)、《教授之屋》(*The Professor's House*)、《岩石陰影》(*Shadows on the Rock*) 等 20 餘部小說問世。1922 年出版的《滄海一粟》(*One of Ours*) 則獲頒普利茲小說獎。

語言貼切精準、角色刻畫細膩是凱瑟作品的特色。她擅長以寫實的手法呈現傳統的價值觀，為隱身世間角落或邊陲的小人物出聲。故事憑藉層層細節，鮮活地迸裂出靈動的人物，引人入勝。在《保羅案例：一樁青春氣質的研究》裡，薇拉 · 凱瑟極富戲劇張力的寫作技巧，呈現出藝術之美與力，和蒼白乏味人生形成強烈對比。她堅持細節的鋪述需要如鑽石琢磨，適度的鑲嵌在內容中，璀璨發光；反對作品中的素材編織如目錄般堆疊，味如嚼蠟。她尤其憎惡對肉體和感官經驗的過度描述。

在文學史上，薇拉 · 凱瑟被銘記為擅長雕塑特定時間、氛圍和地域的說書者。少女時期成長的內布拉斯加大草原，成了許多她的小說裡鮮明的圖景。她琢磨最深的是在二十世紀初，冒險到荒野披荊斬棘，在艱苦環境中掙扎生存的捷克與瑞典的新移民。《噢，拓荒者！》、《我的安東妮亞》和《鄰居羅斯奇》(*Neighbour Rosicky*) 裡，她彰顯了大草原的粗獷樸拙之美、表露出人性堅忍不拔的光輝。許多故事的素材和人物都緊扣著她的成長過程，她相信醞釀在心中良久，經過歲月淬煉的事，透過筆端鋪述在紙上，事不論渺小或偉大，皆是文學。此外，她堅信文學創作簡潔的重要：化繁為簡是所有藝術創作至上的原則。學者大多同意薇拉 · 凱瑟是美國文學二十世紀前半葉的重要小說家。

▲位於內布拉斯加紅雲市的薇拉 · 凱瑟紀念草原。

凱瑟年表

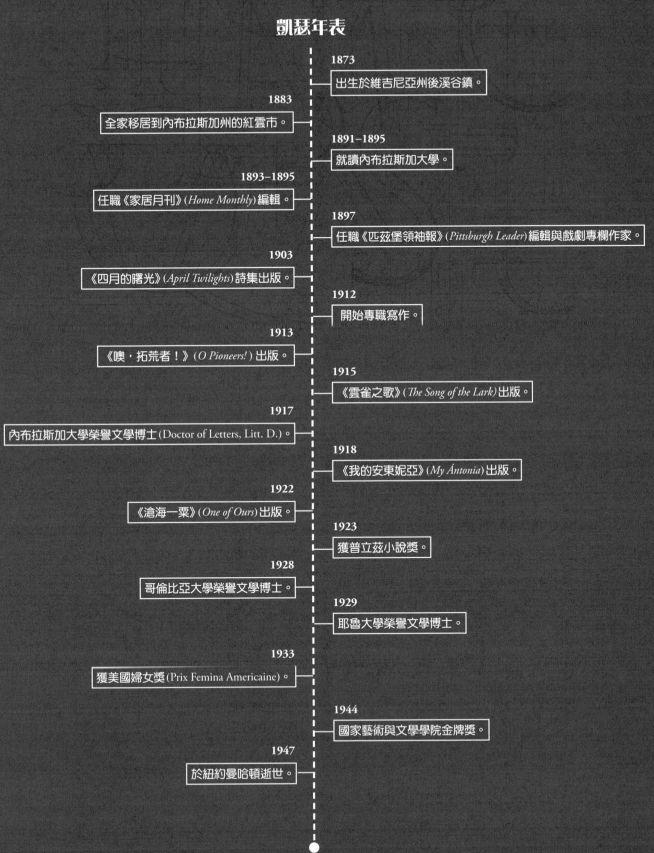

1873
出生於維吉尼亞州後溪谷鎮。

1883
全家移居到內布拉斯加州的紅雲市。

1891–1895
就讀內布拉斯加大學。

1893–1895
任職《家居月刊》(*Home Monthly*) 編輯。

1897
任職《匹茲堡領神報》(*Pittsburgh Leader*) 編輯與戲劇專欄作家。

1903
《四月的曙光》(*April Twilights*) 詩集出版。

1912
開始專職寫作。

1913
《噢，拓荒者！》(*O Pioneers!*) 出版。

1915
《雲雀之歌》(*The Song of the Lark*) 出版。

1917
內布拉斯加大學榮譽文學博士 (Doctor of Letters, Litt. D.)。

1918
《我的安東妮亞》(*My Ántonia*) 出版。

1922
《滄海一粟》(*One of Ours*) 出版。

1923
獲普立茲小說獎。

1928
哥倫比亞大學榮譽文學博士。

1929
耶魯大學榮譽文學博士。

1933
獲美國婦女獎 (Prix Femina Americaine)。

1944
國家藝術與文學學院金牌獎。

1947
於紐約曼哈頓逝世。

課文朗讀 完整 Track 6／分段 Track 6-1

Paul felt annoyed with his father and disliked his plans for him. His father was a hardworking businessman in Pittsburgh, the steel capital of the world. Paul, however, was not interested in business. He did not like his father's old-fashioned* value of hard work and narrow-mindedness. Instead, he loved art, music, and the theater.

Paul felt frustrated with his school. He didn't like his teachers or the classes; he didn't like playing the game of homework and tests; and he thought his classmates were not sincere and did not express their true feelings. Since Paul acted **disrespectful**[2] and broke the rules, the principal and teachers discussed whether to **suspend**[3] him from the school for some time. The principal asked Paul to attend a meeting to discuss his case. At the meeting, Paul wore strange clothes, like an artist—he did not wear the neat and modest clothes that would be suitable for this meeting. He also wore a bright red **carnation**[4] in his buttonhole; this made many of the teachers unhappy. To them, the red flower indicates Paul's disrespectful, carefree attitude. Tall and smiling, Paul looked proud, but his narrow shoulders and large nervous eyes made people feel that he was suffering.

It was difficult for the teachers to talk about Paul. They felt Paul disliked them and looked down on them. They all **criticized**[5] Paul at the meeting, but Paul showed no emotions. He seemed to be lost in his own thoughts and smiled during their various attacks and **criticisms**[6]. After the principal let Paul leave the room, the drawing teacher reported that Paul's mother had died in Colorado soon after he was born. After he spoke, the drawing teacher recalled seeing Paul fall asleep in class one day. When he

---

Something You Should Know

Paul entered the faculty room, suave and smiling. His clothes were a trifle outgrown and the tan velvet on the collar of his open overcoat was frayed and worn; but, for all that, there was something of the dandy about him, and he wore an opal pin in his neatly knotted black four-in-hand, and a red carnation in his buttonhole. The latter adornment the faculty somehow felt was not properly significant of the contrite spirit befitting a boy under the ban of suspension. ("Paul's Case: A Study in Temperament," 1905)

　　保羅異於常情的行為和心理，顯示了他的自我和外在環境之間的距離。他在校園中無法和同學順暢交流，大家認為他不合群；老師要求的學習和課業，他不能如期完成，而且不時以冷漠的眼神待之，著實令老師錯愕困惑。他不合時宜的老舊服裝、特殊的飾針和康乃馨的搭配，讓旁人覺得突兀，但他仍一派從容自在。校方準備處理他的「異端行為」，請他到場說明辯解，他依然一副事不干己。他的穿著和應對，的確會讓外人不解。這些情節預示人的內心與外界存在著無法跨越的鴻溝。

was about to wake Paul up, he looked at Paul's face and felt surprised at how worn out* Paul looked for his age. After some discussion, the **faculty**[7] members decided to let Paul continue his studies. When the teachers left the meeting, they regretted that they had spoken so harshly about their young student.

However, Paul wanted to be suspended. He wanted to leave the school for a while. After the meeting, Paul went to work as an **usher**[8] at the Music Hall in Pittsburgh. He felt excited to work in the world of music and to wear an usher's uniform.

Words for Production

1. temperament [ˈtempərəmənt] *n.* [C] [U] 氣質、性情
2. disrespectful [ˌdɪsrɪˈspektful] *adj.* 不尊敬的
3. suspend [səˈspend] *v.* 停學
4. carnation [karˈneʃən] *n.* [C] 康乃馨
5. criticize [ˈkrɪtɪsaɪz] *v.* 批評
6. criticism [ˈkrɪtɪsɪzəm] *n.* [C][U] 批判；指責
7. faculty [ˈfæklti] *n.* [C] 全體教師
8. usher [ˈʌʃɚ] *n.* [C] 引座員

Words for Recognition

*old-fashioned [ˈoldˈfæʃənd] *adj.* 過時的
*worn out [ˈwornˈaʊt] *adj.* 極度疲憊的

Idioms and Phrases

1. look down on sb 輕視

★★★ Discussion

Paul's strange clothes and the red carnation bothered his teachers so much. Do you think it was fair? Why do you think that to them a flower could mean Paul's bad attitude?

課文朗讀 分段 Track 6-2

In high spirits, Paul went straight to the Music Hall and visited the Hall's art **gallery**[9]. He admired the paintings of Paris and Venice. He felt amazed by a painting called "blue Rico." After signing up for the job, he changed into his usher uniform. Paul was a diligent usher and performed his job well, paying attention to every detail. One evening, he felt annoyed when his English teacher showed up and he had to take her to her seat. He felt that she was not dressed properly for this great music hall.

During the concert, Paul's spirit swam along with the classical music and the powerful **rhythms**[10] excited him. Afterwards, he followed the lead female singer to her hotel, dreaming he was her date. As if suddenly awakened from a dream, Paul realized he was standing alone in the dark on a cold, rainy street corner. He didn't want to go back to his room at home with its **shabby**[11] furniture. Paul began to feel unhappy about his very common neighborhood. He didn't want to face his father, so he entered the house through a basement window. He stayed awake in the basement all night. He was

---

Something You Should Know

‧‧

　　薇拉 ‧ 凱瑟在〈保羅案例〉故事中提到的「藍色瑞克」(blue Rico)，指的是西班牙畫家馬丁 ‧ 瑞克 ‧ 奧爾特加 (Martin Rico y Ortega, 1833–1908) 一系列以蔚藍天空為背景的畫作。薇拉 ‧ 凱瑟在作品中，並未明確提到保羅欣賞的是哪一幅畫。經過學者艾利奧特 (Mary J. Elliott) 的查證，她指出凱瑟分別在 1895 和 1897 年，在卡內基學院博物館內，親眼見過瑞克的〈運河上〉(On the Canal) 和〈威尼斯 ‧ 聖特羅瓦索〉(San Trovaso, Venice) 兩幅畫作。文中 blue Rico 指的應該是瑞克後者以威尼斯為主的畫作。在鑑賞畫作的藝評裡，薇拉 ‧ 凱瑟評論：「我們見到大師瑞克，在略顯肅穆的畫布上，為威尼斯添染幾分喜悅之情：迎接朝陽的聖特羅瓦索、湛藍的天空、映襯著波光粼粼的運河、白紅相間的磚舍、橋及鳳尾船。畫面的左前矗立著黑楊樹，那是兼具大悲和大喜兩種特性的樹。隱然聽到翠綠如碎銀的葉子窸窣作響、隨風在陽光下搖曳。」

　　「藍色瑞克」在故事裡包涵幾層意義。藍色除了代表無垠的天空，也象徵心情的抑鬱沉悶。猶如〈威尼斯 ‧ 聖特羅瓦索〉裡的黑楊樹，象徵悲喜兼備的樹。人性亦復如此，表裡善惡、是非黑白，貌似遙遠的兩端，其實是一體的兩面。人若多點包容和體諒，也許會減緩摩擦與衝突，或許也可以阻止類似保羅悲劇的發生。

▲〈威尼斯 ‧ 聖特羅瓦索〉(San Trovaso, Venice)

afraid that if he made a sound on the stairs, his father would mistake him for a thief on the stairs—and shoot him.

The next afternoon, Paul relaxed on the front **porch**[12] with his father and sisters. The neighbors were all outside enjoying the fine weather, while Paul disliked it and felt **distressed**[13] that his father was chatting with a young office worker who lived nearby. Paul's father thought the young office worker was a good example for Paul. What's worse, this office worker had taken his chief's advice and married the first woman he met and soon had children. His father's business stories bored Paul, but he did love his tales about the adventures of the rich in places like Cairo, Venice, and Monte Carlo! Paul knew that hardworking office boys could work their way to the top and become rich, too, but he would never work so hard like them.

Back at school, Paul lied to his classmates that he was good friends with some famous actors and singers. Paul's classmates didn't like him bragging and ignored him; so he soon became isolated. The principal called Paul's father to tell him about Paul's problems at school. Paul's father could not understand Paul's behavior. At the end, Paul's father took him out of school and stopped him from going to the Music Hall and the theater.

Words for Production

9. gallery [ˈgælərɪ] *n.* [C] 畫廊
10. rhythm [ˈrɪðəm] *n.* [C][U] 節奏、韻律
11. shabby [ˈʃæbɪ] *adj.* 破舊的
12. porch [pɔrtʃ] *n.* [C] 門廊
13. distressed [dɪˈstrɛst] *adj.* 憂慮的

Idioms and Phrases

2. mistake . . . for . . . 把…錯當成
3. work one's way to the top 逐步達成；晉升

★ ★ ★
Discussion

How do different settings, such as at school, at home, in the Music Hall and in the gallery, help us understand Paul and his personality?

Feeling frustrated and trapped, Paul ran away from home and took the night train to New York City. After he reached New York, he went shopping and bought expensive clothes, hats, shoes, and silver jewelry. He then checked into New York's best hotel, paying in cash. Paul bought some flowers to brighten up the room.

Where did Paul's money come from? Had he found it? Did an admirer at the Music Hall give it to him? The truth was nothing like this. After leaving school, Paul began to work at Denny & Carson's, a company. The other day, he was asked to make a deposit at the bank. He found that there were more than two thousand dollars in checks and one thousand in cash. No one knew that he deposited the checks but kept the cash. He then returned to the office and asked for a full day's holiday on Saturday. His vacation in New York was being paid for with stolen money!

After a rest, Paul **strolled**[14] slowly up Fifth **Avenue**[15]. He admired the colorful flowers in the shop windows. Then he returned to his hotel to have lunch, enjoying the soft waltz* played by the hotel band. He felt completely at ease. On the next day, Paul met a college student from a rich family. They enjoyed each other's company, so they went out that night to have some fun. They started the night but soon felt tired and unwell.

On the eighth day after his arrival in New York, Paul read about his **theft**[16] in a Pittsburgh newspaper. The report said that his father had paid the money back and was going to New York to look for him. Knowing his adventure in New York would soon

---

Something You Should Know

. . . .

The carnations in his coat were drooping with the cold, he noticed, their red glory all over. It occurred to him that all the flowers he had seen in the glass cases that first night must have gone the same way, long before this. It was only one splendid breath they had, in spite of their brave mockery at the winter outside the glass, and it was a losing game in the end, it seemed, this revolt against the homilies by which the world is run. Paul took one of the blossoms carefully from his coat and scooped a little hole in the snow, where he covered it up. Then he dozed a while, from his weak condition, seemingly insensible to the cold. ("Paul's Case: A Study in Temperament," 1905)

作者運用康乃馨代表青春年少的新鮮、美麗、敏感和脆弱。花朵會因天冷而凋謝枯萎，燦爛美麗不再；而懵懂無知的孩子常常編織美好、幻想的世界，殊不知它經不起現實環境的打擊，很快就會破滅，化為烏有。保羅在故事的開端，身上別著康乃馨。臨死前，他在雪地挖出小洞將它掩埋。這些行為象徵他保有一顆純真潔白的心，鮮豔燦爛如花，遺憾不被理解，或遭外人誤解。康乃馨象徵愛、迷戀與獨特，恰巧呼應保羅的憧憬。而在服飾上別康乃馨，也可解讀為他可能有特殊性別意識的暗示。

be over, Paul got dressed, put a red carnation in his buttonhole, and went down to eat an **exquisite**[17] dinner at his hotel. Afterwards, he returned to his room and drank whiskey until late that night.

He woke up late the next morning, feeling sick and blue. The **gloomy**[18] sky outside matched his mood. He stared at the gun he had bought in New York; but, he could not shoot himself. Finally, he took a cab from New York to Pennsylvania. The cab dropped Paul off near a railroad crossing in the countryside. He stood by the train track, as if uncertain what to do next. Paul noticed the carnations he wore on his coat had **withered**[19]. Soon, a speeding train came around the corner. Paul suddenly threw himself down across the tracks in front of the roaring train. At the moment of death, he knew he was "too foolishly impatient and wouldn't see any **exotic**[20] places."

Words for Production

14. stroll [strol] *v.* 散步；閒逛
15. avenue [ˋævənu] *n.* [C] 大街
16. theft [θɛft] *n.* [C][U] 偷竊
17. exquisite [ɪkˋskwɪzɪt] *adj.* 精緻的
18. gloomy [ˋglumɪ] *adj.* 陰暗的
19. wither [ˋwɪðɚ] *v.* 枯萎
20. exotic [ɪgˋzɑtɪk] *adj.* 來自異域的；異國情調的

Words for Recognition

*waltz [wɔlts] *n.* 華爾滋舞曲

Idioms and Phrases

4. check into 登記入住
5. the other day (最近的) 某一天

★ ★ ★
Discussion

After reading this story, how would you describe Paul? Is he lonely or artistic? Is he a rebel, a mentally ill person, a thief and a cheat, or a victim of the society?

一、閱讀測驗 (Reading Comprehension)

( ) 1. Why did Paul's teachers change their minds and let him continue his studies?

    (A) One of Paul's teachers revealed something about him.

    (B) Paul's father begged the teachers to forgive him.

    (C) Paul apologized to the teachers for what he had done.

    (D) Paul's classmates liked him and wanted him to stay.

( ) 2. After Paul arrived in New York City, which of the following did NOT happen?

    (A) He read about his stealing in a Pittsburgh newspaper.

    (B) He took a taxi from New York to Pennsylvania.

    (C) He fell in love deeply with a female college student.

    (D) He checked into the best hotel in New York City.

( ) 3. What can we infer about Paul from this story?

    (A) He admired his father but didn't know how to express his feelings.

    (B) He longed to become a musician and perform at the Music Hall.

    (C) He had difficulty learning how to become a successful businessman.

    (D) He was frustrated with his own life and anxious to lead a better one.

( ) 4. How did Paul feel at the moment of his death?

    (A) He felt grateful to his parents for raising him.

    (B) He felt regretful for committing suicide on impulse.

    (C) He felt hostile to those who hadn't treated him well.

    (D) He felt satisfied because he had been to many places.

二、字彙填充 (Fill in the Blanks)

1. _____ A renowned expert wrote an article to c_____e the government's latest environmental policies.

2. _____ The poor old man now lives in a s_____y wooden house.

3. _____ All the flowers have w_____red because Jane forgot to water them.

三、引導式翻譯 (Guided Translation)

1. 前幾天我在回家途中碰巧遇上一位老同學。我很多年沒有見到他了。

    I happened to meet one of my old classmates on my way home _____ _____ _____. I haven't seen him in years.

2. 這個勤奮的女孩起初是名助理，逐步晉升成了部門經理。

    The diligent girl started as an assistant and _____ _____ _____ _____ _____ _____ and became the department manager.

3. 旅客登記入住飯店時需要出示護照及預約號碼。

    When the travelers _____ _____ this hotel, they have to present passports and reservation number.

賞析

這則故事記述少年保羅成長的經驗。首先，他和家人的關係不睦。母親在他出生後不久即離開人世。父親則忙碌於事業，期待這位少年能正常發展，但卻很少真正關心他。此外，保羅喜歡的是藝術、音樂和劇場。鑑於他生性敏感孤獨，抑鬱寡歡，加上缺少家人的關愛和教師的引導，課業和行為皆得自行摸索應對。可想而知，他心中幻想的世界和無情現實環境之間，存在著巨大的鴻溝。這些多重的因素：包括親子關係，學校教育和自我認知之間橫亙疊合的重荷，最終逼使保羅走入絕境。

保羅和父親表面上相安無事，但兩人卻存在緊張和矛盾的關係。父親鼓勵保羅以鄰居為榜樣，找到好工作，成家立業。但是，保羅卻覺得這樣的生活平淡無趣，人應有更高遠的目標，追求靈性精神的生活。父子平日鮮少開誠布公的溝通，心理難免衍生隔閡和疏離。父親若能耐心聆聽，或及時開導，保羅也許會做出不同的選擇。此外，他在學校也需要輔導。他對學習的興致不高，偶爾還違紀犯禁，頗令學校頭痛。特別為他安排師生座談，他出席時的打扮不像學生：奇裝異服，鈕孔別花。對於老師的指責，他的反應時而輕蔑冷漠，時而恍神迷茫。他的繪畫老師說明保羅的母親早逝，指出他在課堂上睡著，滿臉倦容疲憊的神色。在座老師頗覺內疚，決定讓他繼續留校。

家庭和學校教育對於個人的成長，確實有不可磨滅的影響。但是，人必須有成熟的心智和韌性，才能接受挑戰，臻於至善。紐約之行原是保羅發掘自我之旅的開端。他期待進入世界之都，能在精緻藝術的薰染陶冶下，成為一個有品味和高氣質的人。保羅原先瞧不起無趣平凡的鄰居，嚮往都會文化可以提升他的精神境界。然而，世俗的現實敲碎了他幻想編織的理想。保羅的小世界猶如掛在身上的康乃馨，曾經美麗芳香，時移境遷，終於耗盡青春璀璨的片刻，瞬間枯萎凋零。

故事的標題寓意深遠，值得細究。〈保羅案例〉處理的是一個內在與外在失衡的人物；一樁病理的診斷。小說的副題「一樁青春氣質的研究」，尤具深意。現代讀者可能會將保羅當作患有精神抑鬱症的少年。他心理苦悶，找不到傾訴的對象。他的身心失調和情緒紊亂，想藉叛逆對抗眾人平庸的品味。只是，他的離經叛道並不被認同。他雖喜愛美術和戲劇，實際上他卻不是一位藝術家。他只希望藉由竊取的錢財拜訪紐約，希望都會的洗禮能使他達到高雅美麗的境界。他的追逐固然值得嘉許，但是他利用取巧犯罪的手段實現，的確引人非議。現代讀者得有悲憫寬容的心，重新思考：在這場對抗庸俗社會的抗爭中，他是受害者嗎？是社會還是他自己導致他青春夢想的幻滅？

Chapter 7

"Big Two-Hearted River"

關於作者

厄尼斯特‧海明威 (Ernest Hemingway, 1899–1961) 生活的世代和作品呈現的視境早已成了一則文學傳奇。學者認為，海明威是以中篇小說和短篇故事的形式呈現著稱。

他最精彩的幾部作品，皆以特定的地景烘托成形。包括〈印地安營區〉("Indian Camp") 及〈大雙心河〉("Big Two-Hearted River")，兩作分別以伊利諾州和北密西根州做為故事背景。在第一次世界大戰期間，海明威曾在義大利前線協助紅十字的醫療服務，這些經歷後來構成了《戰地春夢》(*A Farewell to Arms*) 的靈感來源。而《太陽依舊升起》(*The Sun Also Rises*)，也和他派駐巴黎擔任《多倫多星報》(*Toronto Star Weekly*) 通訊記者的經驗息息相關。晚年他移居古巴，度過一段肅穆淡定的生活，這種氛圍貼切地呈現在《老人與海》(*The Old Man and the Sea*) 裡。海明威的文學成就在他摘下諾貝爾文學獎的桂冠時達到頂峰。晚年時飽受嚴重的憂鬱症纏身，最後他舉槍自殺結束自己的生命和創作。

海明威的小說，勾勒的是時代的現象，也是洞悉世間真理的鏡子。他以自然樸實的筆法描繪：戰爭、狩獵、垂釣、飲酒和歡愛等。他的文字猶如圖景呈現，形象立體鮮明，讓人有身歷其境 (the sense of place) 的感覺。他也以這種攝相師式的表達為傲，認為作品理應猶如冰山只顯露出一角，其餘藏於冰山底下，言外之意是期待讀者自行挖掘。

他不只反映他生存的環境，同時也揭示世代的精神面貌。海明威的作品描繪的是1920 到 1960 年代間的世事滄桑，其間處理的主題包括戰爭和苦難。細究情節出現的人物，有些代表二十世紀人類共同的經驗，揭露人在面對精神的荒蕪和失序後的彷徨無助。海明威認為人唯有面對窘境與絕望，才能激發潛能和善良。全力以赴後就算徒勞無功，也不代表人的挫敗。生命奮鬥的過程裡散發出的尊嚴、勇氣和不屈的韌性，即代表人活著的意義。學者常述及海明威小說裡塑造的典型英雄形象皆擁有堅毅和正直的性格。他們關懷的是凡人的福祉，而非高大至上的信念。面對戰爭帶來對文明的崩毀，海明威仍堅持人堅韌不拔的意志能克服萬難。

海明威年表

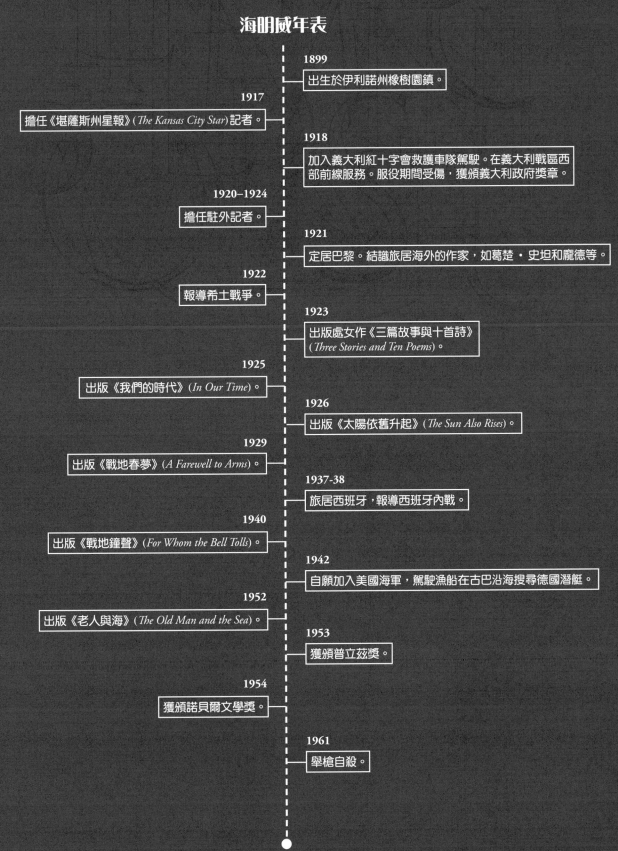

1899
出生於伊利諾州橡樹園鎮。

1917
擔任《堪薩斯州星報》(*The Kansas City Star*)記者。

1918
加入義大利紅十字會救護車隊駕駛。在義大利戰區西部前線服務。服役期間受傷,獲頒義大利政府獎章。

1920–1924
擔任駐外記者。

1921
定居巴黎。結識旅居海外的作家,如葛楚・史坦和龐德等。

1922
報導希土戰爭。

1923
出版處女作《三篇故事與十首詩》
(*Three Stories and Ten Poems*)。

1925
出版《我們的時代》(*In Our Time*)。

1926
出版《太陽依舊升起》(*The Sun Also Rises*)。

1929
出版《戰地春夢》(*A Farewell to Arms*)。

1937-38
旅居西班牙,報導西班牙內戰。

1940
出版《戰地鐘聲》(*For Whom the Bell Tolls*)。

1942
自願加入美國海軍,駕駛漁船在古巴沿海搜尋德國潛艇。

1952
出版《老人與海》(*The Old Man and the Sea*)。

1953
獲頒普立茲獎。

1954
獲頒諾貝爾文學獎。

1961
舉槍自殺。

Nick Adams had taken a train to Seney, Michigan. As the train pulled away, he could see that a big fire had completely destroyed the town. In fact, all of the buildings that had once been there, including the hotel and bars, were now gone.

As he walked over to a bridge, he looked down at the river below. He saw **trout**[1] swimming in the river, and he spent a long time watching these fish. The sun beat down on Nick, but he continued to look at the fish in the river until he finally found a big trout at the bottom of a pool. Looking up, he saw a kingfisher* flying nearby. Then, looking back down at the trout in the river, Nick felt the return of an old familiar feeling.

It was time to move, so Nick picked up his pack and put it on. Though it was heavy, Nick was happy. He began to walk, carrying his fishing **rod**[2] in a case in one hand. Walking with the heavy pack was hard, but Nick felt good to be leaving everything behind. He felt so good that he walked for a long while in the sun, until he had to stop to rest. Smoking a cigarette, he looked out at the burned countryside all around him. Suddenly, an all-black grasshopper* landed on Nick's foot. Smiling, Nick caught it and then let it go.

When he started to walk again, Nick left the road and headed through the forest to the river. He walked until he had to rest again. This time, Nick decided to take a nap. Though he slept for only a few minutes, his body was very stiff after he woke up. Moving slowly, Nick **shouldered**[3] his pack and started walking again. Finally, he came

---

Something You Should Know

··

Nick looked at the burned-over stretch of hillside, where he had expected to find the scattered houses of the town and then walked down the railroad track to the bridge over the river. The river was there. It swirled against the log spires of the bridge. Nick looked down into the clear, brown water, colored from the pebbly bottom, and watched the trout keeping themselves steady in the current with wavering fins. As he watched them they changed their positions by quick angles, only to hold steady in the fast water again. Nick watched them a long time. ("Big Two-Hearted River," 1925)

　　海明威的故事環繞著三要素而成：遠離人群社會、重尋生活準則與自我心理的療傷。故事中許多細節的觀察與意象的鋪述，乃至場景的設定，無不呈現尼克的不安和焦慮。從以上的原文摘錄可看見海明威描寫燒焦的房舍，和滿目瘡痍的風景，讓尼克想起自己在戰場上的殘酷經歷。他希望回到大自然，尋找心靈慰藉，恢復簡單平靜的生活：到野外紮營，獨自處理食物，在河邊釣魚等，是他好好面對並重新認識自己的方法。小說的幾個意象也隱含深層意義：橋是連結此岸到彼岸的空間意象，也是繫接過去，現在和未來的媒介；河流或水既代表時間，也有洗滌心靈、尋得新生的宗教洗禮含意。魚在基督教中代表人，垂釣則象徵排除劫難，承受上帝恩典的感召，暗示重生的可能。

to a meadow close to the river, and he decided to make his camp there.

Setting up his tent and preparing his camp took some time, and when he was done, Nick was very tired. At the same time, though, he felt settled as if nothing could touch him. He knew that this was a good place to camp. He felt he was in his home where he had made it.

By this time, Nick was very hungry, so he started to make his dinner. First, he heated up cans of food in a frying pan, and then he prepared some bread. After he had finished cooking his food, he poured it onto a plate. Nick looked out at a **swamp**[4] across the river as he waited for his food to cool down. Finally, he took a bite of the food, which tasted good. After finishing his dinner, Nick felt like having some coffee. So, he went down to the river and returned to his camp with a **bucketful**[5] of water.

Words for Production

1. trout [traʊt] *n.* [C][U] 鱒魚
2. rod [rɑd] *n.* [C] 魚竿
3. shoulder [ˋʃoldɚ] *v.* 挑起、扛起、承擔
4. swamp [swɑmp] *n.* [C] 沼澤
5. bucketful [ˋbʌkɪtˌfʊl] *n.* [C] 一桶 (量)

Words for Recognition

*kingfisher [ˋkɪŋfɪʃɚ] *n.* [C] 翠鳥
*grasshopper [ˋgræshɑpɚ] *n.* [C] 蚱蜢

Idioms and Phrases

1. pull away (車輛) 開動
2. It is / was time to VR 現在是該 (做)…的時候

★★★ Discussion

Why does Hemingway portray Nick's attempt to achieve a bonding with nature?

課文朗讀 分段 Track 7-2

As Nick started to make his coffee, he thought back to his old friend Hopkins. Shaking his head, Nick remembered that he had argued with Hopkins before about how to make coffee. To honor his friend, Nick decided to make coffee the way that Hopkins had made it. As he waited for the coffee to boil, Nick opened a can of apricots* and began to eat them. Then, when the coffee was ready, Nick poured himself a cup. Drinking the cup of coffee, he thought of Hopkins and all the interesting things that Hopkins had done in the past. Though Nick and Hopkins had once planned to go fishing together in the summer, Nick never saw his friend again.

It was time to turn in for the night. Nick finished his coffee, and he got ready to go to bed. Before entering his tent, Nick thought about how comfortable his camp was. Inside his tent, Nick killed an **annoying**[6] mosquito before he fell asleep.

The morning sunlight arrived early the next day. Nick woke to see the river and the swamp behind it. Though he was excited to start fishing, he knew that he had to eat breakfast first. As he waited for the water for his coffee to boil, Nick decided to go out to collect grasshoppers for bait. He was **fortunate**[7] to find a lot of grasshoppers under a log, and he put the ones he caught in a glass bottle. After returning to his camp, Nick made pancakes. He also made some sandwiches and put them in the pockets of his shirt so that he could eat them later for lunch.

Then, it was time for Nick to fish for trout. He prepared to set out. He took his fishing rod out of its case. The rod was heavy and straight, and as he **threaded**[8] the fishing line, he remembered that he had paid eight dollars for it. Next, Nick opened a

---

Something You Should Know

He had wet his hand before he touched the trout, so he would not disturb the delicate mucus that covered him. If a trout was touched with a dry hand, a white fungus attacked the unprotected spot. Years before when he had fished crowded streams, with fly fishermen ahead of him and behind him, Nick had again and again come on dead trout, furry with white fungus, drilled against a rock, or floating belly up in some pool. Nick did not like to fish with other men on the river. Unless they were of your party, they spoiled it. ("Big Two-Hearted River," 1925)

尼克第一次釣上鱒魚時，他把右手浸到水裡，彎腰用溼漉漉的右手將魚捧起，從魚嘴裡取下鉤子，然後將魚放回河中。海明威在這裡傳達一個重要的「生態環保」概念：接觸魚前得把手弄溼，如此才不會影響魚身上的薄黏液。若是用乾的手去摸，魚身上未受保護的地方就會受到一種白色真菌的侵襲。尼克想起若干年前，不少釣客在溪裡用假蠅為餌釣魚。同時，他見到身長白色真菌，毛茸茸的死鱒魚，漂流撞上岩石或是魚肚朝天地漂浮在水上。尼克覺得和他們一起釣魚十分掃興，這也展現尼克溫柔細心的一面。

box to look at the leaders*. Thinking back, Nick remembered that he had already wet the leaders when he was on the train. Carefully selecting one, he unrolled it, tied it to the fishing line, and fastened a **hook**[9] to the end of it. Then, pulling tight to test the line, Nick smiled with **satisfaction**[10] as he saw that it was working well. To complete the rest of his preparations, Nick hung the bottle of grasshoppers around his neck and his net from a hook on his belt. He also put a large **sack**[11] over his shoulder and carried his fishing rod in one hand. He was ready to start fishing for trout.

Words for Production

6. annoying [ə`nɔɪɪŋ] *adj.* 令人惱怒的
7. fortunate [`fɔrtʃənət] *adj.* 幸運的
8. thread [θrɛd] *v.* 穿線
9. hook [hʊk] *n.* [C] 魚鉤
10. satisfaction [ˌsætɪs`fækʃən] *n.* [C][U] 滿足
11. sack [sæk] *n.* (用麻布等製成結實的) 大袋

Words for Recognition

*apricot [`æprɪˌkɑt] *n.* [C] 杏桃
*leader [`lidɚ] *n.* [C] (釣魚用) 前導線

Idioms and Phrases

3. set out 出發，展開

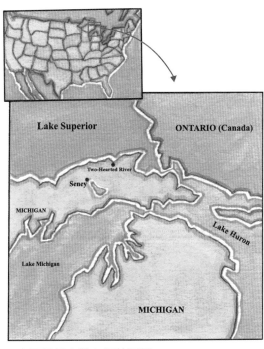

▲密西根州大雙心河位置圖。

★ ★ ★ Discussion

Do you think it effective for Nick to restore himself by escaping into his own world, fishing trout, and spending time by the river?

課文朗讀 分段 Track 7-3

With all of his fishing **gear**[12], Nick walked into the river. The water was cold, and Nick could feel the stones on his shoes as he walked. He opened the bottle of grasshoppers to get one out for bait, but it escaped, falling into the river where it was eaten by a trout.

After putting another grasshopper on the hook, Nick dropped it into the river. Not long after, there was a **tug**[13] on the line. Yes! He had caught his first trout, and he slowly pulled it in. However, this fish was so small that Nick decided to take the hook out of its mouth and release it. While doing so, he made sure that the fish was OK, handling it gently and carefully. In the past, he had seen other fishermen injure the fish they had released. Perhaps this was one reason that Nick did not like to fish with other people.

The fishing continued. Nick saw that the water had only reached his knees, and that he would only catch small fish in the shallow water. He had come to the river to catch big trout, so he moved to deeper water. After putting another grasshopper on the hook and starting to fish again, Nick felt the line suddenly tighten, and he knew that he had a bigger fish on the line. With a snap, however, the line broke, and the huge trout escaped.

His hand shaking, Nick decided to get out of the river to rest. He sat on a log and let his wet pants and shoes dry in the sun. After smoking a cigarette, he found another part of the river to start fishing in again. To his surprise, he quickly caught another big trout, which he carefully **scooped**[14] up in his net. After taking a closer look at the big trout, Nick put it in his large sack and was glad to have caught such a big fish. The

---

Something You Should Know

Nick did not want to go in there now. He felt a reaction against deep wading with the water deepening up under his armpits, to hook big trout in places impossible to land them. In the swamp the banks were bare, the big cedars came together overhead, the sun did not come through, except in patches; in the fast deep water, in the half light, the fishing would be tragic. In the swamp fishing was a tragic adventure. Nick did not want it. He didn't want to go up the stream any further today. ("Big Two-Hearted River," 1925)

尼克曾釣上大鱒魚，卻因線斷裂而讓魚兒溜走。他的手一邊發抖，一邊慢慢收線。從以上原文摘錄可看出，突如其來的挫折令他隱約感到有點不安。釣到大鱒魚代表美好的回憶；鱒魚溜走則暗示美好回憶在現實的世界無法再現。因此，他對於到沼澤地釣魚的反應就顯得遲疑多了。首先，沼澤地深黑難測，加上水底漩渦，雖然大鱒魚在此棲息，對人卻是十分危險。沼澤地猶如尼克的潛意識，那是一處匯聚他的戰爭創傷和一切痛苦回憶的地方。在沼澤地釣魚也是他療癒和終結戰爭苦痛之處，只是他目前心理尚未準備好面對它。但是讀者依稀可以看到，尼克已經逐步拋開戰爭恐怖的陰影，緩緩找到適合他生存的地方。

search for more big trout continued until Nick came across another deep pool. There, another grasshopper was put on the hook and dropped into the water. Not long after, there was another pull on the line. A second big fish had been caught.

At a hollow log in the river, Nick took a closer look at the two big trout he had caught and smiled with pride. He then sat on the log and ate his sandwiches. After his lunch, he smoked a cigarette while looking at the swamp. Though Nick knew he would fish in the swamp **eventually**[15], he also knew that he didn't want to fish there that day. Instead, he **gutted**[16] the fish and put them back in his sack before starting to walk back toward his camp. At the shore, he turned and looked back, saying to himself that he still had many more days left to fish in the swamp.

Words for Production

12. gear [gɪr] *n.* [U] 裝備
13. tug [tʌg] *n.* [C] 拉
14. scoop [skup] *v.* 舀、抱起、拿起
15. eventually [ɪˋvɛntʃuəlɪ] *adv.* 最後
16. gut [gʌt] *v.* 取出⋯的內臟

Idioms and Phrases

4. come across 偶然發現

★ ★ ★
Discussion

In your opinion, has Nick finally regained control of his life in the story?

一、閱讀測驗 (Reading Comprehension)

( ) 1. What is this story mainly about?

(A) How and where Nick fished trout.

(B) Nick's great ability to fish big trout.

(C) What trout stood for in Nick's mind.

(D) Why Nick was so fond of going fishing.

( ) 2. What did Nick use as bait when going fishing?

(A) Shrimps.   (B) Fresh bread.

(C) Small worms.   (D) Grasshoppers.

( ) 3. What's the right order of the things that Nick did the next morning of his camping?

(A) Boiling water → making sandwiches → making pancakes → searching for bait.

(B) Searching for bait → boiling water → making sandwiches → making pancakes.

(C) Boiling water → searching for bait → making pancakes → making sandwiches.

(D) Searching for bait → making pancakes → boiling water → making sandwiches.

( ) 4. What can we learn about Nick from this story?

(A) He liked to start from the deepest parts of the river when going fishing.

(B) He once argued with his old friend Hopkins about how to make coffee.

(C) He usually went to the place he fished trout by taking a long-distance bus.

(D) He enjoyed going fishing with others because they could help one another.

二、字彙填充 (Fill in the Blanks)

1. _____ Jack was f_____e to win the lottery and get a great amount of money.

2. _____ After several years of investigation, the murderer was brought to justice e_____y.

3. _____ Susan smiled with s_____n after she finished the sculpture of a horse.

三、引導式翻譯 (Guided Translation)

1. 公車司機開車前，要求乘客就坐、抓穩車柱或握把。

Before the bus _____ _____ , the driver asks passengers to take a seat, hold on to a pole or a handle.

2. 這個受歡迎的樂團將於明年一月展開世界巡迴演出。

This popular band will _____ _____ a world tour next January.

3. 該是你努力準備期末考的時候了。

_____ _____ _____ to work hard in preparation for the final exams.

賞析

　　故事敘述一位飽受戰爭摧殘和暴力撕裂的年輕人，尼克，如何回歸大自然尋找失落的自我，重新擁抱希望，開啟新的生命。海明威的故事分成二個部分：首先描述尼克療癒傷痕的過程，而後是他對戰爭的回顧和省思。故事運用不同的意象和典故，透過尼克日常生活的經驗呈現，讓自己逐漸拋開戰爭的陰影。他路過慘遭火焚的村屋，而後在路橋上駐足良久，俯首凝視大河與鱒魚。接著他獨自到野外露營，並到河邊垂釣，讓心理慢慢恢復平靜。焚毀的宅邸、乾枯的草地，或變色的蚱蜢，皆象徵戰爭的殘酷和無情。熟悉基督教傳統的讀者，會明白水和魚有濃厚的宗教寓意，藉此暗喻尼克經歷河釣的洗禮，預示他生命復甦的可能。

　　尼克紮營前，曾沿河靜觀環境，希望深入樹林尋得慰藉。他喜歡孤獨，不擅與人相處。在他準備釣魚和涉水的過程，無不表現他淡定的心情。海明威以平鋪直敘的文字，描寫尼克的生活細節與行動，讓讀者於無聲處聽驚雷。平穩細微的敘述點出不帶矯情的精神頓悟。大河在故事的第二部分極為重要：尼克或站在河中，或沿河涉水而行，仔細端詳下游的沼澤。大河成了穿梭在尼克的潛意識和回憶裡的意象。首先，他找到蚱蜢當魚餌。在此，大河象徵尼克的潛意識，捉蚱蜢及紮營任務則代表世俗的井然有序。這一切讓尼克的心情緩緩地沉澱，可以無懼外力的干擾，靜靜地探索自己的潛意識。當他釣上小鱒魚，他知道要維護生態，得把手掌沾溼才能取魚，充分表現尼克對魚和大自然的尊重。接著又有一條大魚上鉤，卻因前導線斷裂而脫逃。原先興奮的心情頓時化為烏有。尼克終於明白在自我發現的時間長河中，人總是會得到東西，卻也會失去一些。誠如《道德經》所言：「將欲取之，必固與之。」

　　隔天，尼克順流而下，深入沼澤區。涉水愈深，潛在的危機也愈多。猶似人向內心深處探索，總有撲朔迷離或不易理解的部分。在故事的最後部分，海明威所勾勒的尼克尚未到沼澤地釣魚。但是細節的鋪述已經暗示尼克的心靈復甦之旅即將開始。沼澤象徵他有意回到戰前簡單純真的生活。但追尋自我的過程，並非風平浪靜。沼澤幽深暗黑，河面常有柳杉樹枝垂下。尼克在此釣魚得十分小心，因為水底的泥淖和湍流裡的漩渦，會把浮在水面上的漂物瞬間捲入河底。而這樣的水域不僅是大鱒魚的棲息地，卻也微妙的觸動了尼克的心靈，他決定改天再來。沼澤代表漆黑幽暗的心靈潛意識，記載著戰爭和戰爭相關的惡夢般的回憶。這裡是尼克療癒和改變戰爭創傷的終極的疆界，他決定下一回合再來嘗試，當他一切就緒，準備妥當。

　　大自然乃人生的教室。日月星辰的循環，萬物化卓的週期，人世間的是非成敗、榮枯盛衰，恆常是宇宙大化不變的真相。尼克面對殘暴的戰爭，留下無盡的傷痛，久難釋懷。讀者追隨尼克沿河穿梭在森林裡，應該對尼克有信心，期待他能逐漸拋開戰爭的恐懼和陰影，儘早在人生旅途中尋得安身立命之處。

Chapter 8

"Barn Burning"

關於作者

　　威廉·福克納 (William Faulkner, 1897–1962) 在二十世紀文壇中是獨樹一幟的作家。他寫出影響力得以跨越世代的長篇小說，短篇故事更以戲劇張力十足、意象編織緊密、主題前後呼應著稱。他一生共出版超過 30 部長篇小說和短篇故事，及若干散文、劇本短論和詩集。

　　福克納的寫實小說，總在平凡處洞悉真相，擅長利用象徵或神話暗示更崇高的真理，揉合歷史、現實和想像於一。時空軌跡的描述，包括第一批移民登陸美洲大陸，繼之以美國內戰，最後還涵納現代南方的新圖象。福克納書寫生活中的衝突，經過現實和歷史的混雜融合，呈現面對困境和挑戰仍願意付出愛與憐憫，並且擁有勇氣與堅毅的個體。

　　此外，福克納在語言、結構和敘述觀點的試驗也值得仔細推敲。他擅用誇飾的語言、冗長的句子、複雜的語法、模糊的代名詞和張揚的形容詞，這些寫作的特點對於讀者的閱讀形成一大挑戰。他將語言和結構融為一體，塑造劈頭直述的敘事技巧，故事不做任何外在的鋪述，直接進入情節，期待讀者將時序和人物自行組合。結構簡單如〈紅葉〉("Red Leaves")，乃至複雜如《聲音與憤怒》(*The Sound and the Fury*)。福克納筆下的敘述觀點多變，從侷限的一人敘事觀點，例如〈那晚的太陽〉("That Evening Sun")，到採用十五名敘事者觀點的《我彌留之際》(*As I Lay Dying*)；而《押沙龍，押沙龍！》(*Absalom, Absalom!*) 則是利用三人的視角拼湊起一個完整的家族歷史傳奇。

　　福克納的故事一般是以時間順序的方式進行，但他也嘗試將古今冶於一爐。福克納的故事兼有想像和真實記憶的勾勒，外在環境的記錄和心靈的探索交叉穿梭，既逼真又震撼。也有評論家認為他的修辭和筆法過度晦澀難懂。持平而論，他處理的主題多元，嘗試運用語言和結構塑造現實，逼近複雜迷離的心靈躍動。福克納擅長故事的發展相互交疊，前後相連。他有些作品合體而觀之，猶如一系列的家族部曲；然而，分而談之又能獨立成篇。福克納的作品，彷彿壁上斑斕的彩色刺繡，各別呈現不同的圖景 (真相)。一旦匯聚，即予人恢弘遼闊的視境。福克納對現代文學的創作影響深遠。

福克納年表

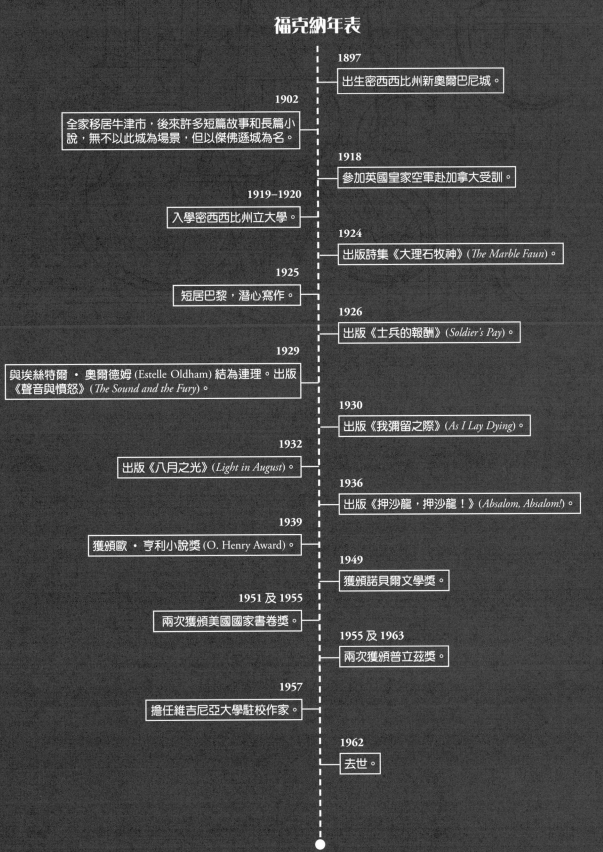

1897
出生密西西比州新奧爾巴尼城。

1902
全家移居牛津市,後來許多短篇故事和長篇小說,無不以此城為場景,但以傑佛遜城為名。

1918
參加英國皇家空軍赴加拿大受訓。

1919–1920
入學密西西比州立大學。

1924
出版詩集《大理石牧神》(*The Marble Faun*)。

1925
短居巴黎,潛心寫作。

1926
出版《士兵的報酬》(*Soldier's Pay*)。

1929
與埃絲特爾 · 奧爾德姆 (Estelle Oldham) 結為連理。出版《聲音與憤怒》(*The Sound and the Fury*)。

1930
出版《我彌留之際》(*As I Lay Dying*)。

1932
出版《八月之光》(*Light in August*)。

1936
出版《押沙龍,押沙龍!》(*Absalom, Absalom!*)。

1939
獲頒歐 · 亨利小說獎 (O. Henry Award)。

1949
獲頒諾貝爾文學獎。

1951 及 1955
兩次獲頒美國國家書卷獎。

1955 及 1963
兩次獲頒普立茲獎。

1957
擔任維吉尼亞大學駐校作家。

1962
去世。

課文朗讀　完整 Track 8／分段 Track 8-1

A ten-year-old boy named **Colonel**[1] Sartoris Snopes, "Sarty," stood in the back of a crowded general store, which was being used as a court. Sarty's father, Abner Snopes, had been **accused**[2] of burning Harris' barn down. It was explained that earlier on, a pig owned by Snopes had eaten some of Harris' corn. And Harris had captured the pig and held it for money. In response, Snopes had sent a black man to pay for the pig but also warned Harris that "wood and **hay**[3] can burn."

Unfortunately, this black man had disappeared. So, Sarty was asked to come forward and tell the truth about what had happened. The boy nervously stated his name and then became quiet. Though he was encouraged to tell the truth, the boy remained silent. He looked at his father, as his family, and Harris, his "enemy." Because Sarty wouldn't speak, the judge stated that there was no **evidence**[4] that Snopes had committed any crime. However, he said that Snopes and his family had to leave town before the end of the day. As Snopes and Sarty left the store, a child called out: "Barn burner!" Enraged*, Sarty hit the boy but was also struck in the face and started to bleed.

Sarty's father pulled him away and told him to get in their **wagon**[5]. Though Sarty's mother tried to clean the blood from Sarty's face, he refused her help. Never looking back, the family left town in their wagon and traveled to a farm in another town. As they traveled, Sarty thought back to the past; this had not been the first time that something like this had happened. In fact, his family had been forced to move to new towns throughout his childhood. The wagon journey lasted for hours until they reached a place

Something You Should Know

"You were fixing to tell them. You would have told him." He didn't answer. His father struck him with the flat of his hand on the side of the head, hard but without heat, exactly as he had struck the two mules at the store... his voice still without fear or anger: "You're getting to be a man. You got to learn. You got to learn to stick to your own blood or you ain't going to have any blood to stick to you..." Later, twenty years later, he was to tell himself, "If I had said they wanted only truth, justice, he would have hit me again." But now he said nothing. He was not crying. He just stood there. ("Barn Burning," 1939)

　　法庭的作證以及庭外和嘲弄他父親的孩子鬥毆，暗示薩地即將面臨的困惑和尷尬的處境：庭上法官要求他作證，正當薩地準備開口承認其父有縱火之嫌，法官便當庭釋放其父；到了庭外一群孩子稱其父是縱火犯，為了替父親辯護，他挺身而出，但卻被打得頭破血流。以上原文摘錄描寫出當天夜晚薩地和父親的簡短交談。他父親重申忠於自己的血緣高於真理和正義維護的重要，並且無端的重捶薩地，警告他不得說溜嘴。薩地明白法庭要的是真相與公理，他說出真相天經地義，但是他父親卻仍堅持血濃於水，家族之名至上。

near a river, where they stopped to camp for the night.

After making a fire and cooking dinner, Sarty was tired and just wanted to go to bed. His father, however, called him over to a small hill. Snopes claimed that he knew that Sarty was going to tell the truth earlier that day. Sarty remained silent, so his father hit him on the side of his head, saying, "You're getting to be a man. You got to learn. You got to learn to stick to your own blood or you ain't* going to have any blood to stick to you. Do you think either of them, any man there this morning would? Don't you know all they wanted was a chance to get at me because they knew I had them beat? Eh?"

Sarty did not cry nor speak. Instead, he just stood there. Snopes **demanded**[6] that his son should answer him, and Sarty only said that he understood. Then, his father told him to go to bed.

Words for Production

1. colonel [ˋkɝnl] *n.* [C] 上校
2. accuse [əˋkjuz] *v.* 控訴
3. hay [heɪ] *n.* [U] 乾草
4. evidence [ˋɛvədəns] *n.* [U] 證據
5. wagon [ˋwægən] *n.* [C] 四輪馬車
6. demand [dɪˋmænd] *v.* 要求

Words for Recognition

*enrage [ɪnˋreɪdʒ] *v.* 激怒
*ain't [eɪnt] 等同於 <u>am not</u>/<u>is not</u>/<u>are not</u>

Idioms and Phrases

1. get at 指責，找麻煩

★ ★ ★
Discussion

How would you describe Snopes' temper in the court house scene?

課文朗讀　分段 Track 8-2

The next day, the family arrived at the new farm, and they started to **unpack**⁷ their things. Sarty's father explained that they would be working there and then said that he wanted to meet the owner of the farm. He told Sarty to come along with him, and they started to walk over to the owner's house.

When Sarty saw the big **mansion**⁸ of the landowner for the first time, he was very impressed. Sarty began to feel peace and joy as he looked at it. However, these feelings quickly disappeared when he saw his father walking ahead of him. Unbelievably, Snopes walked through a pile of horse droppings*, even though he could have avoided them.

At the door, they were greeted by a black servant who told Snopes to wipe his feet before he entered the house. The servant also said that the owner of the farm, Major de Spain, was not at home. **Sneering**⁹, Snopes pushed past the servant and entered the mansion without wiping his feet. His dirty boots made a print on the floor and then left a dirty trail on the clean rug that he walked across. The servant called out for Miss Lula, the wife of the Major, who appeared right away. Sarty was impressed by her beautiful clothing, and the expensive furniture and **decorations**¹⁰ inside the building.

Miss Lula, however, was upset by the dirty tracks that Snopes had left on the

Something You Should Know

The nights were still cool and they had a fire against it... a small fire, neat, niggard almost, a shrewd fire; such fires were his father's habit and custom always, even in freezing weather. Older, the boy might have remarked this and wondered why not a big one... Then he might have gone a step farther and thought that that was the reason: that niggard blaze was the living fruit of nights passed during those four years in the woods hiding from all men... And older still, he might have divined the true reason: that the element of fire spoke to some deep mainspring of his father's being... as the one weapon for the preservation of integrity, else breath were not worth the breathing, and hence to be regarded with respect and used with discretion. ("Barn Burning," 1939)

火象徵多層意義。這把「俐落的微火」(the neat, shrewd fire) 貼切地表現艾伯納謹慎獨特的性格。火也是他報復的工具。他一向慎重其事，非到必要不會輕易使用。福克納利用此段，解釋為什麼艾伯納要焚毀畜棚。艾伯納宿營時的火焰極其微弱，兒子薩地不解其父何以在天寒地凍，仍然維持微火的狀態。當他年紀稍長，第三人稱的敘事者提供兩個理由解釋：美國內戰期間，艾伯納長時間躲藏在樹林裡。他習慣生小火取暖烹煮，此舉可以避免曝露自己的位置。福克納提出另一個理由，也許更具說服力：艾伯納自己宣稱火是「生命深層的動力」，是「維護他完整人格的利器」，他一直「用肅穆審慎的態度」面對。火的威懾之力是艾伯納唯一擁有的力量，任何阻擋或招惹他前行的障礙，他皆會用火解決。

expensive rug. She ordered Snopes and Sarty to leave her home at once. At the gate Snopes stood for a moment, looking at the house. "Pretty and white, ain't it?" He continued, "That's sweat. Maybe it ain't white enough to suit him..." Snopes turned around and left, never looking down at the dirty rug. Sarty had no choice but to follow his father and return to their family.

The owner of the mansion, Major de Spain, was very upset after he returned home. He rode over on his horse and delivered the dirty rug to the family to be cleaned. With little patience, Snopes ordered Sarty to prepare a washing pot, and told his two daughters to start cleaning the dirty rug. Sarty's mother tried to help, but she was told to prepare dinner. Sarty was sent to chop wood, and he returned to find the rug hanging over the stove to dry. When he took a closer look, he could see that although the footprints were gone, the rug had been **ruined**[11].

That night, Sarty slept for a few hours until he was woken by his father. Together, in the early morning, they put the rug on a mule and returned to the mansion to deliver the cleaned, but ruined rug.

Words for Production

7. unpack [ʌn`pæk] v. 打開行李箱、從 (箱、包) 中取出
8. mansion [`mænʃən] n. [C] 宅第、豪宅
9. sneer [snɪr] v. 嘲笑、譏諷
10. decoration [ˌdɛkə`reʃən] n. [C][U] 裝飾
11. ruin [`ruɪn] v. 毀壞

Words for Recognition

*droppings [`drɑpɪŋz] n. [plural] (動物的) 糞便

Idioms and Phrases

2. come along 一起來
3. call out 大聲喊叫
4. at once 馬上

★ ★ ★
Discussion

What do you think prompts Abner Snopes' violent and antisocial (反社會的) behavior?

Major de Spain rode over to the Snopes a little while later. He was very upset about the ruined rug. He said Snopes would have to pay twenty bushels* of corn for the damage. Sarty was upset and told his father that it was not fair that they had to pay so much for the ruined rug. Snopes simply told his son to go and put some tools away.

During the rest of the week, Sarty worked hard at several **chores**[12]. He began to think that all of their problems might simply disappear. Then on Saturday, Snopes, Sarty, and Sarty's brother went into town. There, they went into a store, which was once again being used as a court. Major de Spain was there, and a judge listened to the story of the ruined rug. The judge said that although Snopes did clean the rug, he had also damaged it. As a result, Snopes would have to pay ten bushels of corn to Major.

Upset but not speaking a word about the verdict*, Snopes and his two sons did not return to the farm right away. Rather, they spent the rest of the day in town. Sarty also heard his father say, "He won't get no ten bushels neither. He won't get one." After they ate in town, they returned to the farm.

That night, Sarty woke up to hear his mother begging his father to stop filling the can up with oil. Sarty rushed to them, seeing his father **fling**[13] his desperate mother hard into the wall while she tried to stop him. Snopes then ordered Sarty to go to the barn

---

Something You Should Know

So he ran on down the drive, blood and breath roaring; presently he was in the road again though he could not see it. He could not hear either: the galloping mare was almost upon him before he heard her... he springing up and into the road again, running again, knowing it was too late yet still running even after he heard the shot and, an instant later, two shots, pausing now without knowing he had ceased to run, crying "Pap! Pap!" running again before he knew he had begun to run, stumbling, tripping over something and scrabbling up again without ceasing to run, looking backward over his shoulder at the glare as he got up, running on among the invisible trees, panting, sobbing, "Father! Father!" ("Barn Burning," 1939)

　　這段描述薩地通知德・斯班少校其父意圖焚燒畜棚的經過和其所造成的悲劇。故事中，一旦薩地情緒激昂、詫異，或困惑，福克納即運用相對冗長而複雜的句型呈現。上述的長句子，其中大量使用分詞片語及不中斷的句子，以故事語調的跌宕起伏呈現薩地內心的變化：焦急、恐懼、絕望、悲慟。薩地先是邊跑，還邊閃躲飛奔而來的牝馬。看見夜空染色，顯然父親和哥哥燒了德・斯班的畜棚。接著傳來槍響，薩地開始吶喊「爸爸！爸爸！」看著刺眼的大火，他嗚咽地呼喚「父親！父親！」原先他稱他「爸爸」，如今哀慟莫名，也暫且忘掉其父生前的蠻橫，改以莊嚴的稱謂叫他「父親」。薩地在故事結束前，驀地揣摩其父在南北戰爭時該是位「勇敢的戰士」。

to get another can of oil. Later, Sarty returned and tried to talk his father out of this. Yet, Snopes ordered his wife to hold Sarty down and then took off with his older son. Sarty struggled to free himself, and Sarty's aunt said that they should let him go to warn the landowner. Crying out, Sarty escaped and ran up to the mansion. When he reached the mansion, he yelled out for Major de Spain. Breathlessly, he told Major to go to the barn. Major quickly got on his horse and rode toward the barn at top speed.

Sarty ran away as fast as he could. Suddenly, he heard a shot, followed by two more. He knew that these shots were for his father, and he began to cry, yelling out, "Father! Father!" Finally, he made it to the top of the hill and stopped. He cried even more. Thinking of his father, Sarty sobbed[14] out loud, "He was brave! He was! He was in the war!"

Sarty sat on the top of the hill, cold and shaking. Eventually, he fell asleep. When he woke up, it was almost morning. Sarty was hungry and a little stiff, but he still got up and walked down the hill. As Sarty walked towards the dark woods, he heard birds calling in liquid silver voices. The late spring night was almost over, and Sarty continued to walk, without ever looking back.

Words for Production

12. chore [tʃɔr] n. [C] 日常事務、家事
13. fling [flɪŋ] v. 扔;擲
14. sob [sɑb] v. 啜泣、嗚咽

Words for Recognition

*bushel [buʃl] n. [C] 蒲式耳 (穀物和水果的容量計算單位,約 加侖)
*verdict [ˋvɝdɪkt] n. 判決,裁決

Idioms and Phrases

5. as a result 結果
6. take off 離去,出發

★ ★ ★
Discussion

In your opinion, why does Sarty finally defy his father and try to warn Major de Spain?

一、閱讀測驗 (Reading Comprehension)

( ) 1. Why did Sarty remain silent when asked about who had burned Harris' barn?

    (A) He had no idea who had done it.

    (B) He was afraid of speaking in public.

    (C) He was too horrified to say anything.

    (D) He didn't want to betray his father.

( ) 2. Why did Major de Spain feel very upset after returning home?

    (A) The costly rug in his house was dirty with droppings.

    (B) His servant broke his favorite vase into pieces.

    (C) His wife had left, taking all his treasures with her.

    (D) His mansion had been burnt down in a big fire.

( ) 3. What happened to Abner Snopes in the end?

    (A) He was arrested and then sent to jail.

    (B) He was shot to death by a landowner.

    (C) He left his family, vanishing completely.

    (D) He started a new life on a farm out of town.

( ) 4. What can we know about Sarty's father from this story?

    (A) He was fond of taking his family to wander around.

    (B) He was willing to sacrifice everything for his family.

    (C) He was very hostile toward the rich and landowners.

    (D) He was good at farming and many people wanted to hire him.

二、字彙填充 (Fill in the Blanks)

1. _____ Peter was a_____ed of breaking his neighbor's windows, but he denied doing anything wrong.

2. _____ Sophie couldn't stop s_____bbing when she learned that the trip she had been looking forward to was canceled.

3. _____ The teacher d_____ded her students to turn in their English assignments on time.

三、引導式翻譯 (Guided Translation)

1. Luke 今天上班又遲到了，結果他被老闆訓斥了一頓。

Luke was late for work again today; _____ _____ _____ , he was scolded by his boss.

2. 我們明天要去野餐，你想要一起來嗎？

We are going to have a picnic tomorrow. Do you want to _____ _____ ?

3. 昨天當警報響起時，所有的住戶被要求馬上離開建築。

Yesterday when the alarm rang, all the residents were asked to leave the building _____ _____ .

賞析

　　對於人的尊重是文明的標竿和進步的象徵。寬容、體恤、諒解可以凝結共識，減少衝突。我們理應尊重每一個人享有的基本權利，不論是信仰、膚色、宗教，或理念。尤其不宜將個人的價值觀強加於人；更不該拘泥於傳統的執念做為施暴他人的藉口。福克納的〈畜棚焚毀〉("Barn Burning") 敘說父子對於親情和公義執重的看法分歧，更揭露了脆弱的孩子和無助的母親等的無奈，在父親粗暴蠻橫的威逼下，他們幾乎無法捍衛自己的尊嚴，也失去維護正義的權利。故事最終描述孩子的茫然無助，令人低迴感喟之餘，更多的是哀傷和不捨。

　　故事透過十歲孩子薩地和敘事者的口中，道出薩地日常得面對的兩難：他該認同血緣關係，還是堅持榮譽和公理，忠於自己的良知？薩地和家人對父親艾伯納縱火燒毀畜棚，一直覺得困惑不解，但又無力勸阻。父親一面囑咐薩地有捍衛家庭的責任，卻又常暴力相向，摑巴掌施壓，或怒斥他兩個姊姊動作遲緩。妻子想阻攔他縱火，卻被強力推倒在地。每次縱火時的艾伯納幾近瘋狂，全然喪失對他人的尊重，只是挾怨報復，逞一時之快，不計後果。他全然忘記兒子曾在臨時法庭上為他的無罪辯護。為了證明其父的清白，還與人打架負傷。

　　艾伯納罔顧別人的權益，從另一個事件也看得出端倪，並顯現其白人優越感及種族歧視。他拒絕德・斯班少校宅邸黑人管家的要求，不願抹除鞋底的髒汙，還刻意將馬糞用腳跟揉進毛毯。他冷笑著要黑人管家滾開，還語帶調侃，批評白色的宅邸是黑人的汗水砌成的，而建築似乎還不夠潔白。言下之意，暗指黑人管家別以為住進白人家，就高人一等。他不服管家怎能頤指氣使，要求他抹拭糞汙。畢竟他的皮膚還是黑的，不是嗎？艾伯納心中白人至上的理念早已掩蓋了對人的尊重。他完全不能自省，檢視自己的落魄漂泊來自他的剛烈自負、不願務實面對現狀的態度，他地位的卑微與黑人管家無關。

　　薩地與其他家人期待一個平靜安定的生活。他不解的是：父親何以違逆公理、反對正義和摒棄人權、總是以焚毀畜棚洩恨？因此，在父親最終準備焚燒德・斯班少校的畜棚時，他忐忑不安的心情再次浮現。如今在他眼前只剩下三種抉擇：順從父親，變成他的共犯；或是立即逃家不再回頭；或是試著阻止父親及警告德・斯班少校。薩地最後選擇第三種。只是在通報後，薩地聽見德・斯班少校的一聲槍響，然後又兩聲。福克納小說中並沒有清楚告訴讀者結果如何，但是字裡行間似乎暗示父親和哥哥可能已經命喪槍下。

　　父親容或有諸多缺點，但是薩地絕對沒有想到他會死於非命。原先對父親的恐懼和害怕，現在卻化為絕望與孤寂。薩地心裡除了愧疚和自責，也面臨來日更大的窘境：如今他已無處可去，無人可依。趁著天色微明，他緩緩走入黯沉的樹林，耳際傳來春晨清脆如銀鈴般的鳥鳴，準備迎接新的一天。他踽踽前行，再也沒有回頭。故事雖然結束了，但是福克納卻留給我們無解的人生問題：家庭和正義該如何取得平衡？

Picture Credits

閱讀經典文學時光之旅：英國篇

宋美瑾／編著

文學關懷人生，書寫人生的百態！

精選 8 回經典英國文學名著，帶你遊歷文學的時光之旅！

透過 8 篇不同時代的英國文學作品，讓你在閱讀之後，能領略作者的所思所慮，以及所處時代的價值觀。並且，透過文本引出各項與人生息息相關的議題。希望能夠藉由精挑細選的文學名著，讓你探索人性、擴大自我的視野，同時也能夠提升英文閱讀力！

★ 精選八篇經典英國文學作品，囊括各類議題，如性別平等、人權、海洋教育等。

★ 獨家收錄故事背景的知識補充、原文講解。

★ 附精闢賞析、文章中譯及電子朗讀音檔，自學也能輕鬆讀懂文學作品。

★ 可搭配 108 課綱英文多元選修、加深加廣課程。

Reading Power 系列

Advanced

三民書局

閱讀經典文學
時光之旅：美國篇

解析本

陳彰範・編著

Contents

自傳

　　在十八世紀，班傑明・富蘭克林是一位備受喜愛且鼓舞人心的美國人。他多才多藝，身兼作家、科學家、發明家、慈善家、外交家以及多種身分。他最廣為人知的事蹟，就是在暴風雨中施放風箏，以及簽署獨立宣言。他對世界最重要的貢獻，就是教導世人如何成為一個好人並對社會有所益處。

　　富蘭克林本身就是他教育內容的活榜樣。他只完成了一點學業，在少年時期即離開波士頓，來到費城，口袋裡只有幾個銅板。不過，藉由好運以及辛勤工作，他創造了自己的財富，並在 42 歲即舒適退休。他的《自傳》、《窮理查年鑑》和其他作品給人們信心：任何計畫周詳、努力工作的人都能獲得類似的成功。好幾世代的人們遵循他的教誨，這些教育儼然已成為美國夢的定義。

　　在自我修身方面，富蘭克林制定了 13 項在日常生活切實可行的美德。他計畫一週要努力改善一項美德，並用一期 13 週的時間進行每一項。美德如緘默、決心、節制、秩序、儉僕和勤勞對於引領平衡及有成效的生活極有助益。其中緘默與決心能將你的思緒及言語專注在重要的事情上。節制、秩序、儉僕和勤勞能使你的事情維持井井有條，並讓你保持專注。美德如誠實、正直與中庸則更加深奧，因為在社會上的成功仰賴於贏得人們的信任。最後四項美德是重要的個人習慣，那就是整潔、平靜、貞節及謙虛。如果保持整潔與忠貞，你會感到良好、他人也會更容易接受你。如果你保持平靜沉著，做事即能順利無誤地完成。如果你保持謙虛，即能從他人身上學習。因此，每項美德皆為你的生活提供了實際助益。

　　班傑明・富蘭克林因他的公益精神飽受愛戴與敬重。他創造自己成功的人生同時，也從來沒忘記身邊的人與他居住的地方，美國費城。富蘭克林在公共事務上充分表現了他的公益精神。

　　舉例來說，1727 年，他為想要自我修身的年輕人設立了共讀社，這個社群的成員討論並且實踐富蘭克林的自我修身計畫。1729 年，富蘭克林當上了賓夕法尼亞報的主編，他發行新聞與評論，也提供生活上的建言。在 1731 年，富蘭克林創建了圖書館公司，所以人們可以借書閱讀。在 1736 年，他與他人共同創立了公共消防組織，保護人們與他們的財產不受火災威脅。在 1740 年代，英國正與西班牙及法國打仗，置美國殖民地於危險中。於是，富蘭克林規劃了國民軍防禦賓州。在 1749 年，富蘭克林協助創立了賓夕法尼亞學院，當上院長。學院後來成為賓夕法尼亞大學。最後，在 1751 年，富蘭克林與湯瑪斯・龐德醫生建立了賓州醫院。這是美國殖民地的第一間公立醫院。富蘭克林的公共事務滿足了社會的需求，也展現了他的公益精神。

在他的中年時期，富蘭克林學習如何做科學實驗。他最有名的科學發現就是雷電即是電流。他也發明了避雷針，防止大樓與船隻遭雷擊。因為他對科學的眾多貢獻，英國皇家學會頒給富蘭克林一個代表極高榮譽的獎章。

因為富蘭克林的優秀名聲，賓州政府派遣他前往英國為美國人爭取權益。他的外交能力深受美國人賞識。1776 年，富蘭克林被派到法國，代表美國。在法國，富蘭克林不僅僅是外交官。法國人對富蘭克林個人也深感興趣，包括他的風格與想法。歐洲的科學家與思想家也會拜訪他，與其討論科學與發明。

班傑明・富蘭克林是一個充滿自信與樂觀的人。他相信這些人格特質對個人成就至關重要。在他的作品中，他散布信心與樂觀想法。在公共事務中，他證明了很多公眾需求都能被滿足。他向人們證明若能以信心及清晰思考面對生命中的挑戰，他們應對成功前景感到樂觀。富蘭克林教育內容的基本信念是每人皆有機會作出改進，此信念也成為了美國夢的精神。

美國夢的信念是指只要努力工作、誠實待人，任何人皆能獲得富足、安全與有尊嚴的生活。勤勉工作是前往成功之路，這條路可能漫長，充滿困難，但只要認真工作和把握機會，即有希望成功。

富蘭克林的《自傳》也教導讀者如同對待富有之人一樣，尊重社會底層的市民，因為他們一樣有潛力達到同等的成功。富蘭克林也認為貧窮只有在人不做任何事去改善的情況下是糟的。他更進一步強調，年輕人若無法上學也能自學，激勵了亞伯拉罕・林肯在家自行研讀法律書籍。林肯後來在美國也成為人們無窮盡視野的榜樣。重要的是，富蘭克林的信念讓人們得以在生活困苦時對自我的價值感到自信、對成功感到樂觀；他的教導使人們視美國為充滿機會的大陸。他個人努力與社會責任的信念是奠基美國生活的兩條主軸。

答案

一、閱讀測驗 (Reading Comprehension)

答 1. D 2. A 3. B 4. C

解析：

1. 雖然富蘭克林貢獻良多，但其中最重要的是他教導人們如何成為品行端正及對社會有助益的人，故答案為 (D)。
2. 富蘭克林成立共讀社的目的，是為了要幫助年輕人改善自我，故答案為 (A)。
3. 法國人因為非常賞識富蘭克林，因此才決定要幫助美國，故答案為 (B)。
4. 富蘭克林和湯瑪斯・龐德博士所成立的是全美國第一家公立醫院，不是私人醫院，因此 (C) 的敘述是錯誤的。

二、字彙填充 (Fill in the Blanks)

答 1. beloved 2. accurately 3. worthy

三、引導式翻譯 (Guided Translation)

答 1. rely; on 2. working; on 3. was; remembered; for

翻 譯

最後一個摩希根人

　　廣大的森林如同一個危險而原始的世界延展開來，在這裡，人類的影響微乎其微。黑暗的森林讓遙遠的歐洲戰爭看起來無關緊要。確實，森林讓戰士們極度不安，無心應戰。

　　1757 年，法軍指揮官蒙特卡姆與幾個美洲原住民部落合作，要奪取英國的威廉·亨利堡壘。同時，鄧肯·海沃少校正護送柯拉與愛麗絲前往威廉·亨利堡壘，她們的父親孟羅是那裡的指揮官。在路上，大衛·加蒙，一個天真的基督徒加入他們。接著他們遇見了一位叫做馬瓜的原住民。馬瓜提議要帶領他們到安全的地方，但他卻帶著他們走上了蜿蜒的小徑。

　　過了一會兒，一行人遇見英國軍隊的斥候鷹眼、他的摩希根朋友秦柯古與他的兒子安卡斯。鷹眼不信任馬瓜，他懷疑馬瓜為法國人工作。當他們質詢馬瓜時，他跑掉了。鷹眼猜測馬瓜會再來攻擊他們，於是帶著整個團隊前進到一個島上的祕密洞穴。隔天早上，馬瓜與休倫人攻擊了團隊。

　　他們抓住了海沃、加蒙以及孟羅姊妹。馬瓜承認自己是想找孟羅報仇。奇怪的是，他說要是柯拉答應嫁給他，他就會釋放其他人，但她拒絕了。後來，鷹眼與他的朋友救出他們。一行人小心翼翼地再度啟程前往亨利堡壘，不過他們提防著，怕馬瓜會帶著休倫戰士再度襲擊。

　　他們在夜裡穿過森林。接近亨利堡壘時，他們看見法軍在附近紮營。當接近山坡邊時，愛麗絲聽到她父親下令的聲音。她大聲叫喊著。堡壘的大門開啟，迎接這群人。柯拉與愛麗絲和父親重逢了。

　　法國人攻擊堡壘並且擊敗英軍。海沃接著協助孟羅向蒙特卡姆投降，蒙特卡姆承諾他們能帶著武器與旗幟和平地離開堡壘。

　　第二天早上，英國的男男女女與孩子們和平地步出堡壘。然而，法軍在旁護送時，一個休倫族的戰士試著要從一個婦人身上搶走一條色彩鮮艷的披肩。當她奮力抵抗，戰士就殺了她與她的小孩。馬瓜接著煽動休倫人攻擊英國人，造成了一場大屠殺。在這場混亂中，馬瓜綁架了柯拉與愛麗絲。加蒙則祕密地跟蹤他們。

　　威廉·亨利堡壘成了一片廢墟。安卡斯、秦柯古、鷹眼、海沃與孟羅很擔心柯拉與愛麗絲。海沃發現了他們的足跡，猜測馬瓜抓走了女孩子們。

　　這趟搜救非常辛苦。他們必須小心翼翼，不留下蹤跡，以避開休倫戰士。他們划著一艘獨木舟渡過大湖，然後步行。走過四十英里之後，他們找到人的蹤跡以及剛使用過的營火。馬瓜、柯拉與愛麗絲就在附近。這個夜晚濃霧籠罩，他們遇見了加蒙。

裝扮成原住民的加蒙告訴他們柯拉與愛麗絲還活著，可是被關在不同地方。休倫人讓加蒙自由走動，因為他們覺得他神智不清。海沃裝扮成巫醫與加蒙一起混入村落。這時一組休倫人的部隊剛好抵達，帶了兩個戰俘，其中一個就是摩希根人安卡斯。

海沃偷偷與安卡斯講話，試著要尋找愛麗絲。一個原住民要求裝扮成巫醫的海沃治療他發瘋的妻子，海沃答應了。當海沃被帶到一個洞穴裡去看那個精神恍惚的女人時，一隻熊跟著他進去。為了要騙過休倫族人，海沃開始跳有魔力的舞蹈治療發瘋的女人。接著，那隻熊低吼一聲，拿下他的頭罩，原來他就是鷹眼！海沃告訴鷹眼，安卡斯被抓住了。接著鷹眼繼續以熊的裝扮爬上一棵樹，看到愛麗絲被關的地方。海沃出發去尋找愛麗絲──並向她求婚。馬瓜突然出現在洞穴裡，威脅要折磨海沃，但在馬瓜呼叫支援前，那隻偽裝的熊緊抓住他，海沃把馬瓜綁起來，鷹眼帶著海沃與愛麗絲離開洞穴。

鷹眼帶著愛麗絲與海沃前往友善的德拉瓦村落，接著回到休倫村落，成功地解救了安卡斯。當加蒙和鷹眼接近安卡斯時，鷹眼遞給加蒙一把小刀要他解開安卡斯。接著他們交換服裝。安卡斯穿上獸皮，加蒙穿上安卡斯的便帽和衣服，鷹眼披著加蒙的毛毯，戴上帽子。加蒙待在安卡斯的牢房裡假裝自己是安卡斯。安卡斯和鷹眼離開休倫人的村子，穿過森林，回到德拉瓦村落。

馬瓜在他們到達之前就已經進入德拉瓦村落，並要求德拉瓦族人把柯拉交給他。馬瓜還告訴他們，安卡斯就在他們的村莊裡，而且警告他們鷹眼因為屠殺原住民而惡名昭彰。德拉瓦人召開了一個村民會議，由酋長泰米南主持。此時，柯拉、愛麗絲、海沃與鷹眼也加入了會議。泰米南決定馬瓜能帶走他的俘虜。鷹眼與海沃被綁住，而馬瓜被允許帶走愛麗絲。

泰米南接著注意到安卡斯身上的綠色烏龜刺青，得知他是偉大戰士的後裔。安卡斯勇敢地跳出，釋放了鷹眼，並要求釋放所有的俘虜。泰米南答應讓鷹眼、海沃與愛麗絲自由，可是卻決定讓馬瓜娶柯拉為妻。馬瓜很快地帶著柯拉離開了德拉瓦村落。

現在，秦柯古負責帶領整個隊伍與德拉瓦人一同穿越森林對抗休倫人。他們打敗了休倫人，可是馬瓜卻逃走了，與柯拉藏身在洞穴裡。隊伍跟蹤他，在他們接近時，馬瓜與兩個戰士抓住了柯拉。他們開始爬上山洞另一側的陡峭山壁。

柯拉在山壁突出的狹縫停下，拒絕前進。馬瓜威脅說要殺掉她，可是卻沒辦法下手，另一個休倫人殺了柯拉。安卡斯出現在山崖邊，大吼並殺了殺害柯拉的休倫人。馬瓜從後方刺殺安卡斯，接著他被鷹眼逼到絕境，馬瓜為了逃脫，試著跳下山崖，可是鷹眼射殺了他。

　　在德拉瓦人擊敗休倫人之後，他們為逝者哀悼。孟羅、加蒙以及海沃在柯拉的屍體旁默哀，而秦柯古則坐在安卡斯的屍體旁。

　　在安卡斯的葬禮上，秦柯古表達自己對兒子的愛與悲慟。鷹眼告訴他，安卡斯的靈魂與他同在，而泰米南則宣布：「在我有生之年，我得以看到睿智的摩希根族最後的戰士。」

　　婦女傳頌著柯拉與安卡斯的愛情，希望這對情侶可以在死後重逢。孟羅說：「我們所景仰的神祇會照看我們所有人，不因我們的性別、職位或膚色而有所差別！」鷹眼回應說，人們首先需要互敬互重。在埋葬柯拉與安卡斯之後，歐洲人離開了。不過，美洲原住民的生活似乎也在消逝。

答案

一、閱讀測驗 (Reading Comprehension)

答 1. D　2. A　3. C　4. B

解析：
1. 鷹眼與馬瓜首度見面時，鷹眼並不信任馬瓜，且懷疑他為法軍工作，認為他很可疑，故答案為 (D)。
2. 海沃打扮成巫醫，在加蒙的帶領下混進休倫人的村莊，因此選 (A)。
3. 泰米南在看到安卡斯身上的刺青後，才知道安卡斯的身分，因此選 (C)。
4. 安卡斯是被馬瓜從背後用刀刺死的，並不是被法軍殺害，因此 (B) 的敘述內容是錯誤的。

二、字彙填充 (Fill in the Blanks)

答 1. notorious　2. tortured　3. chaos

三、引導式翻譯 (Guided Translation)

答 1. ran; into　2. cried; out　3. tied; up

翻　譯

白鯨記

　　匹科德號出海，航向南方越過大西洋已經好幾天了，而這艘捕鯨船的船長始終保持神秘，沒有在船上露面。他的名字叫亞哈，大家對他所知的只有一些謠傳，傳說他是個不信神卻又貌似神祇般的人物。他話不多，但說的話都頗具深意。上過大學，也和野蠻人一起生活過。他是個失去了一條腿的捕鯨高手，一直在追捕一隻白色的抹香鯨，叫做莫比·迪克。

　　有一天早上，甲板上響起了亞哈義肢的腳步聲，他頭一次出現在船員面前。橫穿在他臉上的是一條長長的白色傷疤，他所戴的義肢是鯨魚下巴的骨頭做的。他神色肅穆，是個令人不寒而慄的人。藉由恐懼與敬畏，他要所有的船員對他唯命是從。

　　船繼續往南航行，他們接近了鯨魚出沒的海域。亞哈心神不寧，越來越沒辦法待在船長室裡。每到深夜，他經常在甲板上來回踱步，義肢的聲響也不停傳到下面的船員艙房裡，引起了船員的不安。

　　有天，亞哈集合了所有的船員，講了一席話。

　　「各位，你們看到鯨魚的時候該怎麼辦？」他問道。

　　「高聲叫喊！」他們回答。

　　接著他問，「那麼下一步要做什麼，各位？」

　　「放下船隻，追捕牠！」他們吼著。

　　「我們賴以為生的座右銘是什麼，各位？」

　　「不是鯨魚死掉就是船毀掉！」大家激昂地叫著。

　　看著所有的船員表現出上下一心的樣子，亞哈開始講起那隻白色鯨魚。他懸賞一個西班牙金幣給第一個看到這隻鯨魚的水手。大家對他真正的意圖一清二楚，他毫不費力地就讓船員們拋棄了取鯨油的任務，轉而追捕那條讓亞哈受傷的龐大怪物莫比·迪克。現在，所有船員都踏上亞哈的復仇之旅，只有一人除外。

　　「為什麼要找一條笨野獸尋仇？牠也不過是出於盲目的本能攻擊你啊！」星巴克大喊，他是這艘船的大副。

　　「倘若侮辱我的是太陽，我也會痛擊它。」亞哈回應道。

　　所有的船員都動搖了，臣服於亞哈的號召下。他們徹夜狂歡，為莫比·迪克之死而乾杯。第二天，他們下定決心要追捕這隻白鯨。

　　在一個平靜的夜晚，一個船員在船尾工作時聽到了奇怪的聲響，這聲音來自一個船員都不能進去的地方。這不是他們第一次聽到這些奇怪的聲音，也不會是最後一次。有一天，槓杆上的瞭望員看到了一群抹香鯨。「牠就在那邊噴水！」他大喊著。船員們開始行動，把捕鯨艇放下來開始追捕鯨魚。不過，馬上有一群怪異的人從船底跑出來。沒有人看過他們。船上禁區發出來的奇異聲響有了合理的解釋。他們是亞哈的私人捕鯨隊，他在匹科德號出航的前一個晚上把這些人偷偷運上船。有五隊捕鯨員，各自駕著五艘捕鯨艇出發追捕鯨魚。儘管亞哈行動不便及船長很少離開母船的事實，其中一艘捕鯨艇仍是由亞哈親自指揮。星巴克船上的魚叉手貴奎格用魚叉射中了一條鯨魚，可是這兇悍的生物弄翻了船體，逃掉了。這次獵捕沒有成功。

匹科德號往東南方航行，並徘徊於非洲南岸。常常在晚上的時候，遠方會出現一條銀色的水柱，看似是一條鯨魚呼氣噴出來的。不過，不管他們怎麼努力，都沒有辦法趕上這隻鯨魚。有些人說這就是莫比‧迪克在嘲弄匹科德號上的人，引誘他們去追隨牠。他們繼續往東北方航行，沿途注意著這隻白色鯨魚的蹤跡。路途中他們也遇到別的捕鯨船，不過亞哈也只有在能從其他的船隻得知莫比‧迪克的下落時，才會跟他們有所往來。

亞哈繼續追捕鯨魚，讓船員保持忙碌。他不想讓船員去思考，追捕一隻白鯨魚僅為了滿足船長的自尊和權威是否值得。他們順利地抓到兩隻鯨魚，並像其他捕鯨員一樣處理牠們，宰殺鯨魚和取鯨油。

他們再繼續往東航行，莫比‧迪克就在附近出沒的跡象及對船員的影響日益增加。他們碰到了一艘英國的船，山謬‧安德比號。這艘船的船長在捕鯨時，給鯨魚咬去一條手臂。接著，他們進入太平洋以後，就跟瑞秋號聯繫上，在遇到莫比‧迪克之後，這艘船的船長就失去了他的兒子。之後，在與另外一艘叫做喜樂號的船碰頭後，亞哈船長得知他們曾遇上一艘被毀掉的船，這艘船上的四個船員也是因為碰到那隻白鯨而喪命。當匹科德號繼續前行，他們與白鯨的對決勢在必行。

有一天晚上，亞哈突然發現了鯨魚的蹤跡，莫比‧迪克就在不遠處。黎明時刻，亞哈爬上主槓，他爬到差不多三分之二高的地方，就看到一哩外的白色鯨魚。「牠就在那邊噴水！牠就在那裡！像一座雪山一樣的背峰！那就是莫比‧迪克！」亞哈得到他自己的獎賞，那枚西班牙金幣。經過一年的海上生活，他們終於開始追捕莫比‧迪克。他們放下捕鯨艇，開始狩獵。可是，才過不久，這隻鯨魚就潛入陰暗的海洋深處，消失在他們的視線中。起初，亞哈什麼都沒看到。不過當他往海洋深處望去，他看見了白色的一個小點，這小白點慢慢變大，後來變成巨大的物體。毫無疑問，這就是莫比‧迪克，正朝著亞哈的捕鯨艇前來。亞哈試圖轉舵躲開，可是太遲了。這頭猛獸用上下顎把小艇撞成兩半，還好，匹科德號來了，把這隻鯨魚嚇走，沒讓牠殺了亞哈與其他的捕鯨船員。

第二天，他們繼續狩獵。就算前一天發生了那些事，亞哈獵捕這隻鯨魚的決心只變得更堅定。他們看到了莫比・迪克，船員們受到亞哈的決心所鼓舞，跟他一起步入險境。無畏的亞哈迎頭重擊這隻鯨魚，在牠身上插了很多魚叉。鯨魚反擊，衝撞其中一艘捕鯨艇，然後又撞毀另一艘，癱瘓了這兩艘船。只剩下亞哈的那艘小艇還在。而這船上的亞哈跟他的船員，因身處翻騰水中纏亂的繩索與魚叉之間，差點喪命。過程中，亞哈的小艇翻覆了，他也失去了義肢。他又再度被擊倒，很勉強地才逃回匹科德號。

　　「牠在追著我，不是我在追牠——這很不妙。」亞哈說。他最後終於瞭解到，莫比・迪克就是他的終點，不過他還是決定要殺了牠，拼死奮鬥。第三天，他們又看到了這隻鯨魚，亞哈接受了自己的命運，再度登上他的捕鯨艇。這隻鯨魚潛在其他兩艘船之下，毀了它們，而後又再度沉潛於水面下。再次浮現時，莫比・迪克直接衝向匹科德號，直接用巨大的頭撞向船體。船沉了。亞哈拚了最後一口氣，刺向鯨魚，然後就被一條飛來的繩索纏住脖子，拉進海底深處。至於其他船員，匹科德號下沉時的漩渦將他們一起拉了下去。只有一個人存活，訴說莫比・迪克的故事。他的名字是以實瑪利，是此故事的敘事者。亞哈帶著他的狂妄自大，執傲地挑戰自然的力量，但輸了。

一、閱讀測驗 (Reading Comprehension)

答 1. B 2. A 3. D 4. C

解析：

1. 亞哈曾經讀過大學，因此 (B) 所提到的敘述是錯誤的，為本題的正確答案。

2. 船上有一個禁止進入的區域，裡面藏匿著船長的私人船員，所以才會發出奇怪的聲響。故答案為 (A)。

3. 當時許多人捕鯨的原因主要是要去取得鯨油，故答案為 (D)。

4. 以實瑪利是唯一的倖存者，而這個故事是由他訴說，故答案為 (C)。

二、字彙填充 (Fill in the Blanks)

答 1. sneak 2. assembled 3. grim

三、引導式翻譯 (Guided Translation)

答 1. set; sail 2. Out; of 3. making; fun; of

翻譯

歡樂谷傳奇

在十九世紀中期，有一個如理想國般的社區，叫做歡樂谷農莊。一個年輕的詩人邁爾斯‧柯伏道決定要住在那裡。在這之前，柯伏道去看了一場面紗夫人的表演。柯伏道在表演中著迷於一名魔術師的法術，他覺得這神祕的女人似乎擁有預知未來的能力。表演結束後，他又遇到了一個叫做老穆迪的長者。穆迪問柯伏道是否認識一個叫做吉諾碧雅的女人，柯伏道說他並不認識。

在一個很冷的四月天，柯伏道和朋友們前往歡樂谷農莊。抵達時，一名叫做吉諾碧雅的女人迎接他們。她的頭上戴了一朵花，柯伏道立刻被她的美貌吸引。歡樂谷農莊立基於互助、互愛與分享的理念上。有別於當時那些自私又充滿競爭的現代社會，歡樂谷農莊立意要成為現代的「理想國」，在這裡，人們可以回歸簡單、自然的生活，一起努力工作，並活得誠實無欺。

在歡樂谷農莊的成員通常都會一起準備餐點，一起用餐。不過，那天的晚餐卻被柯伏道的老朋友何林沃斯的到訪打斷。他的身邊跟著一個蒼白的年輕女孩。這瘦弱的女孩立刻對吉諾碧雅表示好感，可是吉諾碧雅並沒有回應這女孩的喜愛。最後，女孩說她的名字是普莉斯希拉。

很不幸地，柯伏道生病了，必須休息幾個禮拜。等到柯伏道康復後，他加入其他人在農場裡的工作。他注意到普莉斯希拉身體看起來健康一點了。他也察覺何林沃斯花很多時間與吉諾碧雅與普莉斯希拉在一起。事實上，那時在社區中已經開始流傳有關何林沃斯與吉諾碧雅的流言蜚語，說他們兩個好像是一對。出人意料地，穆迪來到歡樂谷，宣稱自己是普莉斯希拉的父親。他也很關注吉諾碧雅如何對待普莉斯希拉，當他發現吉諾碧雅對普莉斯希拉很好，似乎鬆了一口氣。

過了一會兒，柯伏道出去散步，他在林中碰到偉思特佛教授，這人一直問他關於吉諾碧雅與普莉斯希拉的事情。後來，當柯伏道在「修道院」——一個他想獨處時去的地方——他很驚訝地看到偉思特佛正與吉諾碧雅交談。柯伏道偷聽他們的對話，這對話似乎表明他們過去就認識彼此了。他也聽到偉思特佛說吉諾碧雅應好好處理普莉斯希拉的事情。

一天晚上，吉諾碧雅說了一段叫做「銀色面紗」的故事來娛樂大家。故事中，有個年輕人下定決心要揭發面紗夫人的祕密。他也確實掀開了她的面紗，但她馬上就消失了。接著這故事轉到一名農村少女。少女在樹林裡遇到一個魔術師，魔術師說她命在旦夕，她若要得救，就必須將面紗蓋在她的新朋友頭上，這女孩原是魔術師的囚徒。少女找到她的朋友之後，就依照魔術師的囑咐去做。接著魔術師出現，將面紗夫人帶走。吉諾碧雅的故事說到這裡，她向普莉斯希拉丟了一塊看似面紗的布料，讓女孩非常恐懼。

吉諾碧雅對普利斯希拉的行為極不尋常，但是吉諾碧雅仍經常加入普利斯希拉、柯伏道和何林沃斯到一個叫做艾略特講壇的地方。在那兒，他們常有各式各樣的辯論。舉例來說，吉諾碧雅對女性主義非常熱衷，因此，柯伏道非常驚訝地發現，當何林沃斯做出厭惡女性的評論時，她居然還站在他那邊。而且，普莉斯希拉那時坐在何林沃斯的腳旁，也同意他們兩個所說的事情。很不幸地，柯伏道持續反對周遭的人，尤其是何林沃斯，這人似乎只對利用歡樂谷農莊來達到自己教化犯人的目的有興趣。這兩人很激烈地爭論，導致柯伏道離開了歡樂谷農莊。

柯伏道回到波士頓。在他旅館房間裡，他可以看到旅館對面建築物的房間，有一天，他發現那房裡的人正是偉思特佛、吉諾碧雅與普莉斯希拉。他一直看著他們，直到被吉諾碧雅發現，她很惱怒地拉下窗簾。柯伏道覺得很沮喪，跑到他們的房間。吉諾碧雅來應門讓柯伏道進去。在談話中，柯伏道意識到吉諾碧雅愛上了何林沃斯。普莉斯希拉也出現了，可是吉諾碧雅很快地說，他們另外有約，這三人就離開了。

柯伏道非常困惑，他找到老穆迪。這人似乎比其他人知道更多有關女孩們的事。柯伏道帶老穆迪去喝一杯，想要得到更多資訊。穆迪講述著他的過去，他原名是方特雷洛伊。當他還很富有時，他結婚了，也有一個女兒叫做吉諾碧雅。不過，他失去了財產與家人、生活貧困。後來，他再婚後有了另一個女兒，普莉斯希拉，她有超自然的異稟。穆迪說普莉斯希拉仰慕吉諾碧雅，一心想要和吉諾碧雅一樣。穆迪也透露說，吉諾碧雅的財富來自於穆迪兄弟的遺產。事實上，穆迪才應該繼承這遺產，可是他放棄了這項權利。他答應只要吉諾碧雅好好對待普莉斯希拉，他就把權利讓給吉諾碧雅。

柯伏道聽了穆迪的敘述十分驚訝。他前去觀賞面紗夫人的表演，在那裡，他很驚訝地看見偉思特佛以魔術師的身分站在臺上，控制著面紗夫人。柯伏道很想知道普莉斯希拉會在哪裡。在何林沃斯站上舞臺，呼喚普莉斯希拉時，他很快就得知了。何林沃斯揭開面紗，原來普莉斯希拉就是面紗夫人。何林沃斯接著護送普莉斯希拉離開舞臺，從偉思特佛的手中拯救了她。

柯伏道最後再度回到歡樂谷農莊。然而，在他接近農莊時，一陣不安與焦慮浮上心頭。他在農莊與樹林裡徘徊，來到了艾略特講壇。在那兒，他找到了吉諾碧雅、何林沃斯與普莉斯希拉，他們看到柯伏道都覺得很驚訝。而柯伏道發現何林沃斯與吉諾碧雅似乎不再親密了。吉諾碧雅聲淚俱下控訴何林沃斯愛上普莉斯希拉，這時吉諾碧雅已經承認普莉斯希拉是她的妹妹了。她也宣稱，何林沃斯是因為自己背叛了穆迪，又把普莉斯希拉交給偉思特佛，把財產都輸給了她，何林沃斯才會愛上普莉斯希拉。至於普莉斯希拉，她決定跟著何林沃斯離開，留下吉諾碧雅與柯伏道獨處。

吉諾碧雅崩潰倒地。她絕望地請求柯伏道告訴何林沃斯，他就是那個「謀殺」她的人。吉諾碧雅痛哭著離開，沒有回頭。柯伏道因萬般情緒浮現頗感困惑，他找個地方睡了幾個小時，但卻因心生不祥而醒來。他四處問有沒有人看見吉諾碧雅。她沒有回到農莊。大家組成了搜救隊，何林沃斯、柯伏道，還有其他人後來在河裡找到吉諾碧雅的屍體，她自殺了。

在一個簡單的葬禮之後，吉諾碧雅就葬在一個靠近歡樂谷農莊的山丘上。出人意料地，偉斯特佛出現在葬禮上，他說吉諾碧雅因愛尋短很傻。柯伏道當眾表示反對偉思特佛，儘管柯伏道內心也同意。吉諾碧雅的死是枉然虛擲。他接著看向普莉斯希拉，這女孩似乎仍全心愛著何林沃斯。

幾年之後，柯伏道碰巧造訪何林沃斯與普莉斯希拉。雖然兩人仍在一起，何林沃斯已經放棄初衷，仍對吉諾碧雅的死耿耿於懷。至於普莉斯希拉，她很安靜，但很保護何林沃斯。以她的方式守護這曾經自詡理念堅強，如今卻無力自保的男人，似乎讓普莉斯希拉覺得很快樂。柯伏道自己一直未婚，抑鬱寡歡。他最後表示，他始終都愛著普莉斯希拉。

一、閱讀測驗 (Reading Comprehension)

答 1. C　2. A　3. D　4. B

解析：

1. 歡樂谷農莊的原則中並不包括 self-help (自助)，因此答案為 (C)。
2. 柯伏道之所以離開歡樂谷農莊且返回波士頓的原因，是因為他和何林沃斯的理念不合，兩人經常激烈爭執，所以他才決定離開。
3. 方特雷洛伊就是穆迪本人，並不是穆迪的兄弟，故此敘述是錯誤的，答案為 (D)。
4. 柯伏道後來很不開心，因為他一直都愛著普莉斯希拉，因此正確答案是 (B)。

二、字彙填充 (Fill in the Blanks)

答 1. collapsed　2. terrified　3. reforming

三、引導式翻譯 (Guided Translation)

答 1. turned; up　2. none; other; than　3. dawned; on

翻 譯

頑童歷險記

　　哈克貝利・芬跟他的好朋友湯姆・索耶找到了搶匪埋藏金子的地方，因而一夜致富。銀行找不到哈克的父親，就託管哈克所找到的金子，而哈克也由寡婦道格拉斯領養。哈克・芬與寡婦道格拉斯以及她的妹妹華特生小姐，住在一起，覺得悶悶不樂。他出生於低下階層，沒有受過教育，可是他的新監護人卻一直想要教化他。面對一個乾淨、禮節、學校以及教堂活動的新生活，讓哈克倍感挫折。然而，為了要讓哈克加入湯姆的新「強盜幫」，湯姆要求他讓自己「體面」起來。因此，他盡力依循新監護人所要求的那種像樣的生活。儘管哈克討厭華特生小姐要他嚴守的規矩，還有她強加在他身上的宗教信仰，他還是忍受華特生小姐的蠻橫並保持沉默。除了偶爾忙著跟湯姆還有其他的強盜幫成員惡作劇，哈克逐步適應了學校與家庭的生活。儘管他還是喜歡舊生活，哈克也開始享受這新的人生。

　　直到哈克暴虐的父親回來以前，所有的事情都還算順利。帕普・芬是一個酒鬼，也愛仗勢欺人，他要求拿到哈克的錢。寡婦為了哈克的生活著想，想要得到哈克完整的監護權，可是法官卻判她敗訴。哈克的爸爸死性不改，在城鎮裡四處騷擾哈克。在寡婦告知他遠離哈克之後，帕普惱羞成怒，綁架了他的兒子，把他關在河邊的孤立小屋裡。每次帕普出門的時候，就會把哈克鎖在小屋裡，喝得醉醺醺地回來，有時還會打哈克。這樣的虐待越頻繁地出現，也越來越嚴重，哈克決定必須離開。

　　有一天，哈克找到一艘廢棄的獨木舟，想到了一個簡單而巧妙的辦法。他若是單純離開，他的爸爸還是會緊追不捨，所以他計畫裝死。他先殺了一隻豬，把豬血灑在小屋子裡，讓整個地方看起來像是遭強盜打劫過。接著，他來到河的下游，藏身在密西西比河中央的小島上，看著城鎮裡的人尋找他的屍體。在島上住了幾天之後，哈克碰到了吉姆，他是華特生小姐的奴隸之一。吉姆在知道自己將要被賣到下游的農園時，他覺得自己會受到惡劣虐待，就逃跑了。哈克決定不要拋棄吉姆，相反地，哈克聆聽自己的道德良知，要為吉姆保守祕密。他們兩個一起在島上過著簡單而平靜的生活。

　　有一天，河水漲起來了，兩人看見木筏與房子漂過他們的島。他們拉上這個木筏，並搜索房子，在裡面發現一具屍體，這人是被槍打死的。為了保護哈克，吉姆不讓他看到死人的臉。倒霉的是，哈克得知有人懸賞捕捉吉姆，而且要來搜索全島，他們兩人被迫離開小島。他們用木筏與獨木舟往下游前進。他們想要划向開羅，在那兒他們可以賣掉木筏，搭汽船前往俄亥俄河，到自由的州省，在這些州蓄奴是違法的。就在他們接近開羅的時候，吉姆告訴哈克，他存下賺取的每一分錢，計畫從蓄奴者手中買回妻子與孩子。他還宣稱，要是蓄奴者不願意賣，他甚至會走極端把家人偷回來。

一天晚上，就在他們要去開羅的路上，降下了一陣濃霧，他們兩人分散了。哈克與吉姆花了一晚尋找對方。最後，哈克發現吉姆就睡在木筏上，決定要對吉姆惡作劇。哈克假裝他們根本沒有分開，哈克不過是睡著了。吉姆很困惑，也很生氣，就跟哈克吵了起來，爭論前晚發生的事情。吉姆知道哈克只是胡鬧的時候，他告訴哈克自己有多麼擔心他，在醒來時知道哈克平安無事，吉姆才覺得如釋重負。哈克明白吉姆對自己惡作劇的反應之後，開始認真思考這個同伴的感覺。哈克帶著因戲弄吉姆產生的罪惡感，決定低聲下氣跟吉姆道歉。

在越來越接近自由的時候，吉姆也越興奮與焦慮。哈克這時感到自己正處於道德上的兩難。在他的認知中，他覺得偷走別人的財產是不對的。他決定舉報吉姆。正當哈克在獨木舟上看看是否已經到達開羅的時候，他碰到一隊追捕奴隸的獵人。不過，哈克雖知懸賞的獎金，卻沒辦法把吉姆交給他們。為了掩護吉姆，他告訴奴隸獵人說他的爸爸得了天花。這些獵人害怕被感染，就丟下他們離開了。接著，這兩人發現在大霧中他們已經錯過了開羅，本來計畫要再逆流划回去，也因為醒來發現獨木舟被偷而作罷。這樣的噩運一直持續著，第二天晚上，一艘汽船撞上了他們的木筏，這兩人又再度被分開。

哈克後來成了一個富有人家的貴賓，這家人姓葛蘭福德，他們在哈克與吉姆分開的地點不遠之處有塊很大的領地。哈克盡心享受他與這慷慨的一家人相處的時光，他與這家的男孩巴克成了好朋友。不過事情開始有了極糟的發展。葛蘭福德一家與另外一個家族，薛普德生一家，結下了好幾代的世仇，至於這仇恨怎麼來的，大家也不記得了。這樣的爭鬥，在一個葛蘭福德家的女孩與一個薛普德生家的男孩私奔之後更加惡化。哈克藉著一個葛蘭福德家奴隸的引導，找到了吉姆，而當哈克準備要回到領地時，他看到了兩個葛蘭福德家的小孩無端慘死，其中一個便是巴克。哈克決定要跟吉姆一起回到木筏上，遠離這些紛擾。他們兩個都覺得，河上的寧靜最適合他們的生活。

然而，他們平靜的生活不長，原因是他們從強盜手中救下兩個騙徒。這兩人處處惹事，他們先是欺騙村莊的人看他們的假表演，接著還騙孤女說他們就是她們失散已久的叔叔。哈克認為這些行為是不道德的，就告訴女孩們這些騙徒是一派胡言，想要幫助她們。然後，整村的人都受牽連。哈克離開並回到木筏上，想要擺脫這兩個騙徒，糟糕的是，騙徒隨即尾隨哈克。就這樣，哈克和吉姆就被迫與這兩個討厭的同伴一起旅行。

　　這兩個騙徒最後的惡行就是把吉姆賣回去當奴隸。這時哈克遇到湯姆・索耶，在湯姆的幫助下，哈克決心幫助吉姆重獲自由。

　　儘管他們的計畫成功了，湯姆卻在途中中彈，而吉姆這時沒有逃跑，而在哈克去尋找醫生時留下來照料湯姆。當湯姆自高燒中復原，他知道他們的冒險已經結束了，是時候要跟大家說出他一直隱藏的實情，那就是吉姆本來就已經是個自由人。華特生小姐，也就是吉姆的前任主人，幾個月前就已經過世，她的遺囑中提到要讓吉姆自由。吉姆後來也跟哈克坦白，那天他們在漂浮房子裡發現的那具屍體，就是哈克的爸爸帕普。經歷過這些事情以後，哈克意識到自己不想被教化。哈克逃離他父親是為了尋找自由與新生活，但他在旅途中所見到的殘酷宿怨與欺騙，讓哈克更加珍惜他與吉姆的平靜田園生活和手足之情。他後來也將吉姆當作一個平等的人對待。

答案

一、閱讀測驗 (Reading Comprehension)

答　1. B　2. D　3. A　4. C

解析：
1. 在哈克假裝死亡之後，他藏身在密西西比河中的一座島上，故正確答案為 (B)。
2. 吉姆的主人在過世之前就同意要給吉姆自由並寫於遺囑中，因此正確答案為 (D)。
3. 雖然葛蘭福德一家人對哈克很好，可是他不想捲入兩個家族的紛爭之中，所以決定離開，故正確答案為 (A)。
4. 哈克和吉姆在河上所看見的屍體其實正是哈克的父親，故答案為 (C)。

二、字彙填充 (Fill in the Blanks)

答　1. befriended　2. proclaimed　3. bully

三、引導式翻譯 (Guided Translation)

答　1. came; up; with　2. get; rid; of　3. or; else

Chapter 6
"Paul's Case: A Study in Temperament"

保羅案例：一樁青春氣質的研究

　　保羅對他的父親十分不滿，不喜歡父親為他訂下的計畫。他的父親在匹茲堡是個勤奮的生意人。匹茲堡是世界聞名的鋼鐵大都。不過，保羅對這個事業一點興趣都沒有。他不喜歡父親對認真工作的老舊觀念和狹隘思想。他喜歡的是藝術、音樂與戲劇。

　　學校生活讓保羅飽受挫折。保羅不喜歡他的老師與課程，不喜歡作業與考試，而且他覺得自己的同學們都不真心待人，未曾表達自己內心的想法。因為保羅對師長不敬，又不守規矩，校長和教師們討論是不是要給他停學處分。校長要求保羅出席　個會議，討論他的狀況。在會議中，保羅奇裝異服，像個藝術家，而不是穿著整潔端莊、適合這場合的服裝。保羅還把一朵紅色的康乃馨插在衣服的鈕釦孔裡，這讓他的老師很生氣。對他們來說，那朵紅花代表他的桀驁不馴。保羅身材高大，面帶微笑，外表看來很得意，可是仔細一瞧，他那削瘦的肩膀與緊張的大眼讓人覺得他身陷痛苦中。

　　老師們討論到保羅就覺得十分棘手，他們覺得保羅不喜歡他們、瞧不起他們。他們都在會議中批評保羅，不過他也沒有什麼情緒性的反應。他沉浸在自己的心思裡，對於各種攻擊與批評都一笑置之。在校長請保羅離開會議後，繪畫老師表示，保羅的母親在他出生不久就死於科羅拉多。他還記得看過保羅有天在課堂上睡著。當要叫醒他時，他看著保羅的臉龐，覺得保羅好像年紀輕輕就精力耗盡了。這些老師進一步討論之後，決定讓保羅繼續唸書。老師在散會之後，都後悔自己對這個年輕學生太過嚴厲了。

　　可是，保羅一心想要休學。他想要離開學校一陣子。在會議結束後，他去匹茲堡的音樂廳做引座員的工作，能夠在音樂的世界裡上班，並且穿上引座員的制服，保羅覺得很興奮。

　　保羅覺得精神振奮，直接進入音樂廳，並去參觀音樂廳裡的畫廊，欣賞巴黎與威尼斯的畫作。他被一幅叫做「藍色瑞克」的畫作震懾到了。他在簽到後去換上引座員的制服。他工作勤奮，把事情做得很好，對任何細節皆很注意。一天晚上，他看到他的英文老師來了，覺得十分不悅。他帶著老師入座，並認為要來這偉大的音樂廳聽演奏，她的穿著不甚合宜。

　　演奏會開始後，保羅的心神隨著古典樂起起伏伏，強烈的節奏讓他覺得振奮。

之後，他跟蹤女主唱回去她的旅館，夢想著自己是她的男伴。如夢初醒般，他意識到自己獨自站在雨天街道的陰暗角落裡。他不想回到自己的住處，因為那裡盡是一些寒酸的傢俱。當他回到自己住家的那一區時，保羅對這一切的平庸非常不滿。他不想看到他的父親，就從地下室的窗戶爬進屋裡，清醒地待在地下室一整晚。他很害怕自己如果發出一點聲音，他的爸爸會把他誤認成正在爬梯潛入的小偷，然後射殺他。

第二天下午，保羅到前門門廊與他的父親和姊姊們放鬆休息一下。這時鄰居也都出來享受好天氣，但保羅不喜歡這個景象。看到他的父親跟住在附近的一個員工聊天，他覺得很沮喪。保羅的父親覺得這個員工會是保羅的好榜樣。更糟糕的是，這個員工聽從他的老闆的建議，娶了他才剛遇到的女人，馬上就有了小孩。父親經商的故事讓保羅覺得很無聊，不過保羅卻很喜歡富有人家在開羅、威尼斯，或是蒙地卡羅等地的冒險事蹟。保羅知道，公司裡的小伙子們努力工作，就可以步步高升，財源滾滾，可是他自己沒辦法如此努力工作。

保羅回到學校以後，謊騙他的同學他和名演員及歌手是朋友。他的同學不喜歡他老是大肆吹噓，所以都忽視他，很快地他就被孤立了。校長告訴保羅的父親他在學校的狀況，但保羅的父親無法理解保羅的行為舉止。最後，保羅的父親帶他離開學校，並要他遠離音樂廳和劇院。

保羅覺得自己處處受限，非常沮喪。他逃家，搭上了夜車來到紐約。當他抵達這個城市時，他買了昂貴的衣帽、鞋子還有銀飾。然後他入住紐約最好的旅館，用現金付費。保羅還買了些花來裝飾房間。

保羅的錢是從哪裡來的呢？他找到的嗎？某個在音樂廳的仰慕者給他的嗎？事實完全不是如此。在保羅離開學校之後，他到一家叫做丹尼與道森的公司工作。某天上班的時候，他必須跑腿去銀行存款，他發現居然有超過兩千元的支票與一千元的現金。沒人知道他將支票存入銀行，但自己卻留下了現金。然後，他回到公司並要求隔天星期六要放整天的假。因此，他的紐約之行其實都是拿偷來的錢買單的！

稍作休息之後，保羅在第五大道閒晃。他很喜歡店面櫥窗裡面多采多姿的花。接著他在旅館吃了午餐，欣賞了旅館樂隊演奏的華爾滋。他感到全然放鬆。第二天，他遇到了一個出身有錢人家的大學生，他們享受彼此的陪伴，晚上一起出去找樂子。晚上剛開始玩得盡興，可是他們後來卻覺得筋疲力盡。

在保羅抵達紐約的第八天，保羅在匹茲堡的報紙上讀到他的竊盜案件。根據這則報導，他的父親已經賠償了那一千塊錢，而且要來紐約尋找他的兒子。保羅知道自己的紐約冒險之旅很快就要結束了，他好好穿戴了一番，在鈕鈕孔上放上了紅色康乃馨，下樓吃了一頓旅館供應的精緻晚餐。接著，回到房間一直喝威士忌喝到很晚。

第二天他起得很晚，感覺噁心，也覺得很憂鬱。外面陰沉的天空與他的心情相符。他盯著在紐約買的槍，不過他沒辦法舉槍自盡。終於，他決定搭計程車從紐約到賓夕法尼亞。計程車讓保羅在鄉間的一個鐵路平交道下車。保羅站在鐵道邊，彷彿無法決定接下來要做什麼。保羅注意到自己衣服上的康乃馨已經枯萎了。很快地，一列火車急駛而來。保羅突然跳到呼嘯的列車前，在他死前，他意識到自己是「何其愚蠢地沒耐心，再也看不到那些充滿異域情調的地方。」

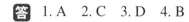

答　案

一、閱讀測驗 (Reading Comprehension)

答 1. A　2. C　3. D　4. B

解析：

1. 當老師們在討論是否該暫時讓保羅停學時，一位教繪畫的老師告訴大家說保羅的母親在他出生不久後就過世，而他曾經看過保羅年紀輕輕就筋疲力竭的樣子，頓時使得在場的老師們感到心軟，最後改變心意，讓保羅繼續他的學業，因此答案為 (A)。

2. 保羅到了紐約市之後，入住最好的旅館、在報紙上讀到了關於他所犯下的竊案的報導、搭了一輛從紐約往賓州的計程車，而且也曾和一位來自富裕家庭的大學生作伴，但是並沒有提到他愛上了一位女大學生，因此 (C) 所描述的事並沒有發生。

3. 由全篇文章內容可以得知，保羅對於自己現在的生活感到很不滿意，一直響往著更有品味、更好的生活，因此答案為 (D)

4. 保羅在死亡那一刻覺得自己過於愚蠢、缺少耐性，而且還沒去過那些充滿異域情調的地方，可以判斷他對於自己衝動自殺的行為覺得很後悔，正確答案為 (B)。

二、字彙填充 (Fill in the Blanks)

答 1. criticize　2. shabby　3. withered

三、引導式翻譯 (Guided Translation)

答 1. the; other; day　2. worked; her; way; to; the; top　3. checked; in

翻 譯

大雙心河

　　尼克 · 亞當斯搭上火車前往密西根的錫尼小鎮。當火車離站時，他可以看到之前被大火摧毀的城鎮。事實上，曾在那矗立的建築物，包括旅館與酒吧，現在都已消失了。

　　在他走過橋的時候，他往下看看腳下的河流和在河裡游來游去的鱒魚。就這樣，他看著這些魚良久。就連烈日當空下，尼克仍然一直看著河裡的魚，直到他看到了一條在河底的大鱒魚。他抬頭看到翠鳥在附近飛翔。接著，他又低頭看著河裡的鱒魚，尼克感到此時此景似曾相識。

　　該動身了，尼克拿起背包並背上。儘管負擔沉重，尼克還是感到很快樂。他開始往前走，手拿著裝在匣子裡的釣竿。背著沉重的行李行走確實不易，不過尼克因為揮別了過去而感到愉悅。帶著怡然的心情，他在太陽底下走了好些時候，然後停下來休息。一邊抽著菸，看著四周一片焦土的郊區景色。突然之間，一隻黑黝黝的蚱蜢停在尼克的腳上，尼克笑著抓住牠，又將牠放走。

　　當他再度動身時，尼克離開了大路，進入森林，來到河邊。他一直走，到了必須休息的時候才停下來。這次，尼克決定要小睡片刻。雖然他只睡了幾分鐘，整個身體卻在醒來時感到十分僵硬。尼克緩慢地背起行囊，繼續前進。最後，他來到河邊的草地，決定在這裡紮營。

　　尼克花了一些時間搭起帳篷、布置營地，做完這些事情，他覺得很疲倦。不過，這時他覺得安定下來了，彷彿沒有什麼事情可以打擾他。他知道，自己找到了一個好地方來紮營，感到非常開心。他覺得自己像是回家了一般。

　　這時，尼克非常餓，就著手開始做飯，首先，他用一個煎鍋加熱罐頭食物，然後準備一些麵包。在他烹煮完成後，就把食物倒進盤子。東西太燙沒辦法吃，等著食物涼下來的尼克往外看去，看到河岸對面的一塊沼澤地。後來，他吃了一些食物，覺得很可口。吃完晚餐之後，尼克想喝一些咖啡，就走到河邊，打了一桶水回來。

　　當尼克開始煮咖啡的時候，想起老朋友霍普金斯。他搖搖頭，想著以前跟霍普金斯爭論過如何煮咖啡。為了向老友致意，尼克決定用霍普金斯的方式煮咖啡。在等咖啡煮沸的時候，尼克拿出一罐杏桃並打開來吃。接著，咖啡煮好了，尼克為自己倒了一杯。一邊喝著這杯咖啡，尼克一邊想著過去霍普金斯做過的趣事。尼克與霍普金斯曾約好了要在夏天一起釣魚，可是他沒機會再見到這位朋友了。

夜晚降臨，該休息了。尼克喝完咖啡，準備睡覺。進去帳篷之前，尼克想著他的營地是多麼舒適宜人。在帳篷裡面，尼克打死了一隻討厭的蚊子，然後就睡著了。

第二天，一早的陽光來臨，尼克醒來，就看到大河與其後的沼澤地。他很興奮地準備釣魚，不過，他也知道自己得先吃早餐。在他等著煮咖啡的水沸騰的時候，尼克決定出去捕捉蚱蜢來當餌。他很幸運地在一塊木頭下找到很多蚱蜢，他把這些小東西都捉進玻璃罐裡。回到營地以後，他做了煎餅。他也準備了一些三明治，放在襯衫的口袋裡，晚一點可以拿來當午餐吃。

接下來，就是尼克要大展身手釣鱒魚的時候了，他準備出發，將釣竿從匣子中取出。竿子又重又直，在他把釣魚線纏上魚竿的時候，想到他曾為這個花了八塊錢。接著，尼克打開一個盒子，看著前導線。他回想著之前在火車上已經把前導線弄溼了。他小心地揀選了一個，把繩子展開來，綁在釣魚線上，並在其中一端綁上鉤子。然後，他把釣魚線扯直，試試看是不是夠牢固。尼克看到這些東西功能正常，很滿意地微笑起來。尼克繼續做剩下來的準備工作，他把那罐蚱蜢掛在脖子上，並將網子鉤上鉤子，掛在腰帶上。他在一邊肩上放上一個粗布袋，一隻手上拿著釣魚竿。他要出發去釣鱒魚了。

帶著他所有的釣魚裝備，尼克走進河中。河水很冷，在他涉水的時候，他可以感覺到鞋子踏過石頭。他打開裝了很多蚱蜢的罐子，拿出一隻來當餌，可是這隻蚱蜢卻逃走了，掉到河裡面，被一隻鱒魚吃掉。

再把另外一隻蚱蜢放上掛鉤，尼克把鉤子甩進水裡。不久，尼克感覺釣魚線有一股拉力。來了！他快要釣到他的第一條鱒魚了，他慢慢把魚拉上來。不過，這條魚好小，尼克決定要把鉤子從魚的嘴裡拿掉，把牠放回河裡。在做這件事的時候，他確認魚沒事，並且盡量輕柔小心地處理這條魚。以前，他曾經看過其他釣魚的人傷了他們要放掉的魚。也許，這也是尼克不喜歡跟其他人一起釣魚的原因吧。

繼續釣魚。尼克看到水深只有到達膝蓋，他知道在這麼淺的水域只能釣上一些小魚。他來到這條河就是為了釣到大鱒魚，所以他就涉入更深的水域。在把另一隻蚱蜢掛上掛鉤之後，他又繼續釣魚。尼克感到線突然被拉直，知道有大魚上鉤了。不過，經過這麼猛力一扯，線斷掉了，大鱒魚就這樣跑掉了。

尼克甩著手，決定上岸休息一下。他坐在一塊木頭上，在太陽下晾乾他的褲子跟鞋子。抽完一根菸，他找到河流的另外一邊，繼續釣魚。讓他覺得很驚訝的是，很快地另外一條大鱒魚就上鉤了，他很小心地把魚捧進網中。尼克看著這條大鱒魚，把牠放到大粗布袋裡，想到能釣到這條大魚，就覺得很開心。他繼續尋找其他的大魚，來到了另外一個深潭。在那兒，尼克將掛在鉤上的另一隻蚱蜢丟進水裡。沒過多久，另外一股拉力出現，第二條大魚上鉤了。

坐在河流中的一個中空木頭上，尼克仔細地看著他釣上的兩條大魚，他驕傲地笑了。接著，他坐在木頭上吃起三明治。用完午餐後，他抽了一根菸，看著那片沼澤地。雖然尼克知道自己遲早要進入那片沼澤釣魚，但不想當天進去。他回頭處理好那兩條大魚的內臟，再把中空的魚放在大布袋裡，然後走回營地。在岸上，他回頭看看，跟自己說，要進去沼澤地釣魚，來日方長。

答案

一、閱讀測驗 (Reading Comprehension)

答 1. A　2. D　3. C　4. B

解析：

1. 本文主要是關於尼克釣鱒魚的過程以及地點，因此答案為 (A)。
2. 尼克是用蚱蜢當作魚餌，因此答案為 (D)。
3. 在第二天早上，尼克先煮水以準備泡咖啡、外出尋找魚餌、製作煎餅、最後是製作三明治，因此正確答案為 (C)。
4. 尼克曾經和他的老友霍普金斯爭論如何泡咖啡的事，因此 (B) 的敘述是正確的。

二、字彙填充 (Fill in the Blanks)

答 1. fortunate　2. eventually　3. satisfaction

三、引導式翻譯 (Guided Translation)

答 1. pulls; away　2. set; out　3. It; is; time

畜棚焚毀

有一個叫做薩多里斯上校 · 斯諾普斯 (小名薩地) 的十歲男孩，正站在一間擁擠的雜貨店後方。這間店面要被用來當作法庭。艾伯納 · 斯諾普斯，薩地的父親，被控燒毀哈里斯先生的畜棚。根據他們稍早的解釋，斯諾普斯的豬吃掉了哈里斯的穀物，而哈里斯抓走豬好用來追討贖金。斯諾普斯派了一個黑人去贖回這條豬，同時警告哈里斯說「木頭與乾草容易著火」。

很不幸地，這個黑人不見了。因此，法庭招喚薩地做證人，說出事情的經過。這孩子緊張地輕聲說出自己的名字，然後就保持緘默。雖然大家都鼓勵他說出實情，這孩子仍然不說話，他目視他的家人父親，以及「敵人」哈里斯。由於薩地不願開口，法官宣布斯諾普斯的犯罪證據不足。不過，他也要求斯諾普斯一家在當天離開城鎮。當斯諾普斯與薩地要離開店面的時候，一個小孩喊著：「燒畜棚的！」薩地很憤怒，打了這個小孩，不過也被反擊，被打到臉龐淌血。

薩地的父親把他拉開，叫他上馬車。雖然薩地的母親想要清理他臉上的血痕，薩地卻斷然拒絕。這一家人就這樣一去不回頭，駕著馬車要去另外一個城鎮的農場。旅途上，薩地回想著過去，這也不是第一次舉家遷移。事實上，在他童年時，他們家就一直被迫遷往新城鎮。馬車走了幾個小時，他們來到了河岸邊，停下來紮營準備過夜。

起火埋鍋造飯之後，薩地累了，想要休息，可是他的父親卻叫他去小山丘那兒。斯諾普斯說他知道薩地在當天稍早想要說出實情，薩地沉默了，他的父親打了他的頭，說：「你要像個男人。你要學會教訓，學會忠於自己的家族，否則家族不會忠於你。難道你覺得今天早上那些人會替我們家著想嗎？你難道不知道，因為我已經整倒了他們，他們現在都在找機會整倒我？哼？」

薩地沒有哭，也沒有說話。他只是站在那兒。斯諾普斯要求兒子回答他，薩地也只是說他了解了。然後，他的爸爸叫他去睡覺。

第二天，他們來到了農莊，停下來拆解行李。薩地的父親解釋，他們將要在這裡工作，他要去見農莊的主人。他要薩地隨他一道去，他們就一起走去農莊主人的住處。

當薩地第一次看到農莊主人的宅第時，他印象深刻，感到一陣陣的平靜與喜悅迎向他來。然而，在他看到父親走在前面時，這感覺很快就消失了。令薩地驚訝的是，斯諾普斯踩上一坨馬糞，其實他本來應該可以避開的。

走到門口，一個黑人僕役出來招呼他們，要斯諾普斯進門前把腳擦拭乾淨。這個奴僕也告訴他們，農莊主人，德・斯班少校，並不在家。斯諾普斯冷笑著推開僕役，也沒把鞋子擦乾淨就進到房子裡面。他的髒靴子在門上與他走過的地方留下了髒腳印。僕役呼喊少校的妻子蘿拉小姐，女主人出現了。薩地看到她的漂亮衣服，還有房子裡面昂貴的傢俱與擺飾，覺得嘆為觀止。

不過，蘿拉小姐看到斯諾普斯留在昂貴地毯上的髒腳印，覺得很生氣，她命令斯諾普斯與薩地立刻離開她的房子。在大門斯諾普斯停了一下，看著屋子。「又美又潔白，不是嗎？」他繼續說道：「都是汗水蓋成的。也許對他來說還不夠潔白呢，配不上他……」斯諾普斯轉頭就走，對於他留下的髒腳印不屑一顧。薩地只好立刻跟著父親回去找自己的家人。

豪宅的主人，德・斯班少校，回家後非常生氣。他騎著馬，帶著這條髒毯子要求斯諾普斯一家人清理乾淨。斯諾普斯很不耐煩，叫薩地準備清潔的水盆，然後命令女兒們清理這條髒毯子。薩地的媽媽想要幫忙，不過斯諾普斯叫她去準備晚餐。薩地則是被叫去砍柴，回來就看見那條毯子已被掛在爐子上晾乾。不過當他靠近一點仔細看，卻發現雖然腳印洗掉了，整條毯子也毀損了。

那晚，薩地睡沒幾個小時，就被父親叫醒。在清晨，這父子倆將毯子放上騾子，要把這件洗好卻已經完全被毀掉的毯子還給大宅主人。

一會兒後，德・斯班少校騎馬去找斯諾普斯一家，他因為毯子遭毀非常氣憤，他說斯諾普斯必須要付出二十蒲式耳的玉米來賠償他的損失。薩地很不高興，他跟父親說要為一條壞掉的毯子賠這麼多很不公平，他的父親只是要他去將工具收好。

在那個禮拜，薩地努力工作，處理種種家務，他以為所有問題應該都消失不見了。禮拜六時，薩地跟他的父親與哥哥進到城裡。他們走進一間再度被充當法庭的店面，德・斯班少校在那兒，還有一個法官正在聽毯子遭損毀的前因後果。法官說，雖然斯諾普斯清理了毯子，確實也將它弄壞了。所以，斯諾普斯必須賠償德・斯班十蒲式耳的玉米。

斯諾普斯對於這個判決非常不服，卻也沒說什麼。他們那天並沒有直接回去農莊，而是整天都待在鎮裡。薩地也聽到他的父親喃喃自語地說：「他不會得到這十個蒲式耳，一個都不會。」他們在鎮裡用餐之後，就回到了農莊。

那天夜裡，薩地醒來，聽到他的母親苦苦哀求著父親不要在瓶子裡面灌油。薩地跑去找他們，目睹他的父親將絕望、想要嘗試阻止他的母親推去撞牆。斯諾普斯這時命令薩地去畜棚拿另外一罐油。過了一會，薩地拿回來了，他也想勸父親不要這麼做。斯諾普斯給他的回應卻是要母親制住薩地，而後就與大兒子離開了。薩地拚命掙扎，薩地的阿姨也說應該要放掉他、讓他去警告屋主。薩地哭喊著掙脫了束縛，跑向那幢豪華的宅第。當他抵達時，他喊著要找德・斯班少校，上氣不接下氣地告訴德・斯班少校趕快去畜棚。德・斯班騎上馬，全速衝過去。

薩地用盡全力逃離現場。突然之間，他聽到了一聲槍響，後來又出現兩聲。他知道這幾槍打的就是自己的父親，薩地開始哭泣，哭喊著：「父親！父親！」最後，他跑上山頂，止不住自己的哭泣，嗚咽出聲：「他很勇敢！很勇敢！他參加過內戰！」

薩地坐在山頂上，因寒冷而發抖。最後，他睡著了，當他醒來的時候，幾乎已是清晨。薩地很餓，身體有些僵硬，不過他還是起身走下山丘。當薩地走向黑暗的樹林時，他聽見銀鈴般不絕的鳥囀。晚春的夜晚就要結束了，而薩地繼續走著，不再回頭。

答案

一、閱讀測驗 (Reading Comprehension)

答 1. D 2. A 3. B 4. C

解析：

1. 由文中第四段的內容以及後續發生的事件來判斷，當初放火燒哈里斯家畜棚的人應該是薩地的父親，而薩地在法官面前之所以保持沉默，是因為他不想說出事實來背叛父親，所以答案為 (D)。

2. 當德・斯班少校返家後看到家裡的貴重地毯上面沾了糞便，覺得非常生氣，因此答案為 (A)。

3. 由文中倒數第二段的描述以及之前故事的情節來推論，薩地的父親最後應該是被德・斯班少校開槍殺死的，而德・斯班少校是一位有錢的地主，因此答案為 (B)。

4. 由文中提到薩地父親的種種行徑來推論，他應該是一個敵視富人和地主的人，所以才會故意去和這些人作對並惹惱他們，因此合理答案為 (C)。

二、字彙填充 (Fill in the Blanks)

答 1. accused 2. sobbing 3. demanded

三、引導式翻譯 (Guided Translation)

答 1. as; a; result 2. come; along 3. at; once

英文讀寫萬試通

我的第一本英文主題閱讀書

- 本書由車畇庭審定，三民英語編輯小組彙編。
- 適用於學測、指考、全民英檢初、中級。
- 全書共 16 回，前 3 回分別解說初、中、高階閱讀技巧，後 13 回仿大考閱測題型。
- 附解析本，含文章翻譯、完整答題思路與答題模板。
- 學校團體訂購附 3 回贈卷，供教師即時驗收學生的學習成效。

閱讀焦點
快速聚焦每篇學習重點！

閱讀技巧
針對閱讀焦點、條列解說閱讀技巧，
口語、系統化說明讓教學零負擔。

常見的題目類型
貼心彙整近六年大考高頻率閱測題型，幫助建構學生答題資料庫。

歷屆試題示範
提升大考應變力！

量身打造！
本書可搭配加深加廣選修課程「英文閱讀與寫作」，讓教師無縫接軌新課綱、教學輕易達標！

八篇故事，八篇有關勇氣、野心、迷失與療癒傷痕的美國經典文學

　　美國文學相較其他國家，崛起甚晚。早期作品多自歐洲文學的風格延伸而來，爾後也觸及社會狀況，描寫殖民時期的美國、戰爭的苦痛與慘烈、黑人於白人社會的掙扎等等。文學刻劃出當代複雜情勢，勾勒出虛偽或善良的人性，反映人們奔放或壓抑的心理。

　　本書選文涵蓋十八至二十世紀，空間廣納城市、鄉村，及海洋。描述時代遞嬗之下，當代人民的希望與苦難——文學並不難懂，文學就是另一個時代的你和我。透過閱讀，你我得以跨越時空，一窺那已無法觸及的世界。

★ 可搭配 108 課綱英文多元選修、加深加廣課程。

★ 精選美國經典文學作品，囊括各類議題，如性別平等、人權、海洋教育等。

★ 獨家收錄故事背景的知識補充、原文講解。

★ 附精闢賞析、文章中譯及電子朗讀音檔，自學也能輕鬆讀懂文學作品。

三民網路書店
www.sanmin.com.tw

「閱讀經典文學時光之旅：美國篇」與「解析本」不分售
80714G